About the Author

Susan Price won the Carnegie Medal for *Ghost Drum* in 1987 and was shortlisted again in 1994 for *Head and Tales*. She writes: 'I was born in a slum in Oldbury, West Midlands – no bathroom or running water inside; an outside lavatory shared with several other households; and cockroaches and mice. But we got a council house when I was four, and moved about a mile away, nearer to Dudley, where I still live.

I have a pet, a little grey tabby cat with white patches. She has beautiful pale green eyes, with a black line round them, as if she is wearing mascara. I like sharing my house with another kind of animal. I always have to share my chair with her. Tig's usually curled up somewhere near me while I'm writing.'

Also by Susan Price

Telling Tales
The Wolf Sisters
The Story Collector
Hauntings
The Bone Dog

Other Signature titles available from Hodder Children's Books

Blackthorn, Whitethorn
The Flight of the Emu
THE MOVING TIMES TRILOGY:
Bloom of Youth
Grandmother's Footsteps
Stronger than Mountains
Rachel Anderson

Sea Hawk, Sea Moon
Beverley Birch

Stuck in Neutral
Terry Trueman

Control-Shift
Seed Time
Nick Manns

Elske
Cynthia Voigt

Nightcomers
Susan Price

Hodder
Children's
Books

a division of Hodder Headline Limited

First published in Great Britain in 1997
by Hodder Children's Books

This edition published in 2001

10 9 8 7

A Catalogue record for this book is available
from the British Library

ISBN 0 340 65605 0

Typeset by Avon Dataset Ltd, Bidford-on-Avon, Warks.
Printed and bound in Great Britain by
Clays Ltd, St Ives plc

Hodder Children's Books
A division of Hodder Headline Limited
338 Euston Road
London NW1 3BH

Contents

The Christmas Trees

'Oh look! Look! The chimney sweep! Oh, I used to love him!'

Jennifer was holding up a small glass globe which tapered, at the top and bottom, into delicate glass spikes. It was a perfect, pale lavender in colour, neither too red nor too blue. The translucent glass sphere attracted light and held it, like a bubble. Painted round it was a dark-blue silhouette of a chimney sweep carrying a long ladder on his shoulder, and another silhouette of an old-fashioned lamp-post. White blobs of snow fell around the sweep, and there was a suggestion of snow-covered ground at his feet.

'This was one of the globes I had when I was a little girl,' Jennifer said, holding the delicate bauble above the heads of her own two daughters, Anna and Catherine. Anna reached up for it.

'No, let Catherine hold it, and you can look at it. Be careful, Cath, it's very fragile. I'm amazed it's still in one piece.'

'I've always kept 'em packed up well,' Brenda said. She was Jennifer's mother, and the girls' grandmother. 'Here's another two, look, the Moons.'

'Oh, the Moons! Oh look, the Moons!'

Now Jennifer held, one in each hand, two long crescent moons made of coloured glass. One was a dark blue, the other a dark red, and they had faces painted on them.

'I must say, your tree is very good,' Brenda said. 'I didn't ever think I'd like an artificial tree, but that's as good as a real 'un, that one. Cones and everything.'

Jennifer had packed the artificial tree in the car, along with the clothes for herself and the girls, and the presents.

'It even feels like a real tree,' Brenda said, shaking her head.

'Can I put this one on?' Catherine asked, holding up the chimney-sweep globe. 'I'll be careful.'

Her mother nodded, and they all watched as Catherine hung the first globe on the tree: the old, fragile chimney-sweep globe that Jennifer had once had hung on her trees.

'Let me put one on!' Anna shouted.

'All right, all right.' Her mother delved into the big old cardboard box, with wine bottles printed on the side, in which her mother had kept the Christmas decorations for many years. 'Oh look! Sputnik!' She held up an odd, spiky silver ball, dangling from a cotton loop. It was made of plastic, so Anna couldn't break it. 'You hang that on.'

'What's a sputnik?' Anna asked.

'Oh, now you've asked me something!' Jennifer looked at her mother, who shrugged. 'I think it's something to do with

2

space – I think it was a Russian space satellite, years ago. I don't know if that's really meant to be a sputnik – that's just what we always called it. Oh look!'

Catherine laughed. 'You keep saying that, Mom! "Oh look! Oh look!" '

'Well, I keep seeing all these old friends. Just look!' She held up a model giraffe, made of a frosted white plastic, which sparkled as it twisted from its fine cotton loop. One of its legs had been broken off.

Catherine laughed again. 'A giraffe! A three-legged giraffe! What's a giraffe got to do with Christmas?'

'Didn't one come to the manger?' Brenda asked.

'Oh Gran!'

'Let me put another on!' Anna demanded.

'You hang on the ones we brought with us, my love,' her mother said, handing her a plastic box. 'They're all yours. You can hang every one of those on the tree wherever you like.' To her mother, as Anna very solemnly set about her task of choosing exactly where each of her ornaments should hang, Jennifer said quietly, 'Ours are all plastic. She can't break any of them.'

Anna took gold and silver filigree spheres of plastic from her box, while Catherine found, among the tissue paper and tinsel in her grandmother's box a candle of coloured glass: a glistening, frail red stem of hollow glass, topped with a glass flame of yellow, with a little grey metal grip at the bottom, to fasten it to the tree. Anna was lifted on to a chair by her grandmother, to place silver and gold plastic pears and apples in the higher branches. Catherine, with breathless care, took a silvery-blue glass bird, with a long shimmering tail of white glass-fibre from among the rustling tinsel in the box. She wagged it in front of her little sister's face, to make it shine, and stroked her cheek with the soft tail. Anna tried to snatch it, but Catherine kept it out of her reach. 'You tell me where to put it: you choose where it goes.'

Dipping again into the big cardboard box, Catherine lifted out a blackened string, hardly thicker than a cotton thread. Clinging to it here and there were little worms of spongy white stuff. 'What's *this*?' she asked in distaste.

'Oh *that*!' Her grandmother took it from her. 'Now *that* is old-fashioned tinsel.'

'*Tinsel?*' Catherine said. The nasty looking stuff didn't shine at all.

'Oh, it was quite pretty when it was new,' Brenda said. 'I bought this – oh, dear-oh, it was some years ago now. Before your Mom was born—'

'What, in medieval times?' Catherine said.

Her mother gave her a mock-threatening look as she helped Anna fix a tricky globe to the tree.

Brenda pulled a strand of Catherine's hair. 'What does that

make me – prehistoric? I bought that tinsel when your Uncle Andy was born, I think. It tarnished after a few years, went all black like this. These modern materials am marvellous.' She picked up a long, thick trail of deep crimson tinsel, which waved and shimmered along its length. 'We had nothing like this back then. None of these colours – and this keeps for years and years, good as new. I do like to see it all hanging in the stores.'

'Do you remember "Angel Hair"?' Jennifer asked.

'Oh I do!' her mother said, and they both laughed. Seeing Catherine looking puzzled, her grandmother said, 'It was this white stuff I bought one year. It was like all soft – white – like fine—'

'It was glass fibre,' Jennifer said.

'Was it?'

'It was glass fibre, spun very fine,' Jennifer explained to her daughters. 'And you spread it out and spread it out over the tree until it was like cobwebs, and the lights shone through it and went all rainbow-coloured. Oh, I loved that stuff.'

'Is this it?' Catherine had dived back into the big cardboard box and had come up with a tuft of something like very flimsy white hair. Her mother took it from her and rubbed it between her fingers.

'That must be a bit of it, yes.'

'Do you think—' Catherine was elbow deep in the box again. 'Do you think we could find enough of it, in bits, in here, and put it all together and—' She broke off. 'This box *smells* like Christmas.'

Her mother came, leaned over the box and sniffed. 'It *does!*' It was a smell of pine, and of something harder to name – of cold, from the cold back room where the box was stored and, somehow, of old glass and old sweets, and winter. But though there were shreds and wisps of Angel Hair everywhere in the box, clinging to old globes, there wasn't enough to drape over even a couple of branches.

'Oh look!' Jennifer cried, pouncing. From a nest of tinsel she lifted out an old grey egg-box. She lifted the lid to show what it was filled with – 'They're real, painted egg-shells, so you must be very careful – careful, Anna! They'll break ever so easily.' She lifted one out of the box by its loops of embroidery silk. It was painted with red toy soldiers and teddy bears. A long tassel of embroidery silk hung down from its bottom. 'They're real, blown egg-shells.'

'I remember you making 'em,' Brenda said.

Anna, who had hung all her ornaments on the tree, came pushing up. 'Who made them?'

'We did,' Jennifer said. 'Me, and your Uncle Andy, and your Auntie Ceel – because so many of our old globes had been broken and we hadn't got much money to buy any more, so we made some of our own. Your Uncle Andy painted this one; he was really good even then.'

Catherine lifted another of the globes. It was painted a dark, metallic bronze, and covered with a design of silver tendrils, vine leaves and grapes, and hung on a loop of gold embroidery silk, with a gold tassel hanging below.

'Your Aunt Ceel did that one – and that one, the one with the silver cockerel—'

Anna made a grab for the egg-box, and Catherine snatched them out of her way, just in time. Anna gave a squeal of rage.

'Would you like a mince-pie?' Brenda asked, bending down to her. 'You come on with Granny and we'll see if we can find some mince-pies. Would you like a glass of something?' she asked Jennifer.

'I would, I'd love it – it's about time I got pie-eyed, I think. I painted that one with the cockerel,' she said, as her mother and youngest daughter left the room hand in hand.

Catherine lifted the painted egg. It was black, with a crimson loop and tassel. The cockerel was painted in silver, while on the other side of the egg were some words about the bird of dawning singing all night long. 'It's lovely,' Catherine said.

'It's not bad,' her mother said. 'But your Auntie and Uncle were always better than me. Still, there's some painted by all of us. I'd hate 'em to get broken.'

'They ought to be kept – for ever,' Catherine said. 'Handed down. They're beautiful.'

'I don't think they'll last for ever. They're only egg-shells.'

7

'They've lasted this long.' Catherine hung the silver cockerel on the tree, choosing a place where it could easily be seen. 'If we look after them, they'll last.' She moved one of Anna's plastic pears in order to hang the egg painted with vines in its place. '*They're* only out of shops,' she said. 'These eggs should be in the best places.' She got on the chair and moved another of the plastic globes to the back of the tree, where it wouldn't be seen. 'Pass me up the one with the teddy-bears on it.'

Brenda came back in, carrying a tray with a plate of home-made mince-pies and cakes, two glasses of wine, and two glasses of orange juice. Anna followed, eating a chocolate-chip cake. She began fumbling about in the big cardboard box, hardly able to reach to the bottom of it. Since all the most fragile ornaments had been taken out, and there were only plastic ones and tinsel left, no one stopped her. Standing on tip-toe to reach to the bottom of the box as it stood on a low coffee-table, she lifted something high into the air, sending strands of tinsel flying, and demanded, 'What's this?'

It was a bundle of wires, a sort of broom-head of bare, spiky wires.

'Ooh, mind! You'll have your eye out!' Brenda cried, trying to find somewhere to set the tray down quickly.

Jennifer took the wires from Anna.

'Well, I never,' Brenda said. 'It's mother's old tree.'

'What – Gran's?' Jennifer asked.

'Yes, your gran's.' Having wedged the tray on the edge of the table, she took the bundle of wires from Jennifer and began opening them out until they took on the shape of a small, crude Christmas tree – an ugly, bare little Christmas tree with a trunk of thick wires twisted together, and branches made of long spikes of thinner wire. 'This belonged to my mother,' she explained to her granddaughters. 'To your mother's grandmother.'

Catherine, still standing on the chair, with a long strand of golden tinsel in her hands – shining, modern tinsel – pulled a face and said, 'It's not much of a tree.'

'Oh, it didn't look like this when it was new.' Still holding the little wire tree, Brenda sat down in an armchair. 'All this wire was covered in silver tinsel when I bought it for her. It was one of the very first artificial trees, when they never tried to make 'em look like real trees. I suppose they couldn't.'

Anna sat down on the floor and took another cake. Catherine climbed down from the chair and chose a mince-pie. Jennifer picked up her glass of wine.

'Me mother – her'd be your great-grandmother – her lived to be a very old lady. Oh, her did love Christmas. Her always wanted a tree. But it was too much for her when her was old and living on her own – too much money, too much trouble with the pine needles and all that. So I bought her this little tree one year. I used to visit her every day, to see her was getting on all right, and every year on the first of December, her'd get it out and set it up on her sideboard.'

'Here's its stand,' Catherine said. From the bottom of the box she took out a stand of red plastic and fitted it together. She took the tree of bare wires from her grandmother and fitted it into the stand, and stood the tree on the coffee table.

'Her didn't mind it not looking like a real tree,' Brenda said. 'Her loved anything shiny, me mother, and it was all silver tinsel when it was new. I bought her a set of tiny little globes, all different colours – they'm still about somewhere, and her loved to put 'em on it. And when her got really frail, and couldn't really do much for herself, her'd be on at me, as soon as it was November, "It'll soon be time to put me tree up." And her'd keep on, more and more – by the end of November her'd be on at me all the time. "Get me tree out the cupboard and put it up." Her couldn't bear to wait longer than the first of December. It had got to be put up. And there it'd stand on the sideboard until Twelfth Night, and her'd sit and look at it. We used to put her presents round its stand. Her really loved that little tree.'

Catherine began to sift through the tinsel still left in the big cardboard box. While her mother and grandmother sat back in their armchairs and sipped their wine, and while her sister steadily ate her way through the pies and cakes, Catherine sat on the rug and patiently wound gold and silver tinsel around the bare wires of the little tree. The two women were too busy talking, and Anna too busy eating as much as she could while no one was watching her, to take any notice of what Catherine was doing, until she stood the little tree upright on the table and said, 'There!'

'Oh Cathy!' her grandmother said.

The little tree looked better than it ever had, decked out in brighter and more luxuriant tinsel than it had ever sprouted before, shining and shimmering, now gold, now silver.

'Twelve Princesses!' Anna shouted.

The two women looked puzzled. 'What's her say?' Brenda asked.

Catherine was used to interpreting for Anna. 'There are trees with branches of gold and silver in the "Twelve Princesses". You know – the fairy story.'

'It looks better than new!' Jennifer said, admiring the glittering little tree. She sounded surprised, as if she hadn't thought her daughter capable of having the skill or patience to do such a thing.

'Where are the little globes for it?' Catherine asked. 'You said you still had them.'

'Now wait a minute.' Brenda began to get up. 'I think I know exactly where to look for 'em.'

Catherine, kneeling by the table, lifted her mother's glass and looked at her mother, who nodded. So Catherine sipped

11

at the wine, liking its warmth and trying not to shudder at the bite of the alcohol and the bitterness under the sweetness. Anna came begging for some, and Jennifer said she might have a sip too. 'Just a little sip – now, that's enough now, that's enough for a little girl.'

Brenda came back into the room, carrying an old chocolate box and a little framed photograph. 'That's my mother, look, that's your great-grandmother.'

Catherine took the photo, which was black and white. It showed a tall, thin woman with a big smile, wearing a flowery frock and leaning against a wall.

'That was taken in Blackpool,' Brenda said. 'Her used to love Blackpool as well. Went every year, to see the illuminations. Her loved bright colours and anything shiny.'

Catherine was looking from the photograph to her grandmother and her mother. 'She doesn't look like you – either of you.'

'No, I didn't take after her,' Brenda said. 'I wish I had. Her never had an ounce of fat on her, my mother, and look at me!' Brenda was short and plump.

Catherine put the photograph down on the table and opened the old chocolate box. Inside, tumbled together, were tiny glass spheres, about the size of Maltesers. They were bright, shiny, and intensely coloured: red, green, blue, silver, gold, purple.

'Oooh!' Anna cried, and made a dive for them.

'Careful, careful!' Catherine said. She caught hold of Anna's hand and put into it one of the bright little green baubles. 'Put it on the tree then. Don't be rough. Put it here.'

All the little globes had lost the fastenings that fixed them to the tree, but they all had a hole where they had been. Guided by Catherine, Anna fixed the globe to the little tree by pushing this hole on to the end of one of its tinsel-covered wire branches. Green glass against gold tinsel, it shone.

'My turn.' Catherine took one of the purple globes and poked it on to the end of a silver branch.

'My turn!' Anna shouted, and was about to snatch when Catherine said, 'Ah-ah!' So then Anna slowed down, chose a bright, cherry red globe and pushed it on to the end of a gold branch.

'Oh, it's so pretty,' Brenda said. 'Mother would have loved it.'

Turn and turn about, the sisters went on adorning the little tree. A bright blue globe on a silver branch; a silver globe on a gold branch, red on silver, blue on gold. The little tree seemed to grow bigger, to spread its tinselly branches, to glow and sparkle in the light.

'So pretty,' Brenda said, shaking her head, her voice choking in her throat. 'Oh, listen to me. I must have had more to drink than I thought.'

Also in the chocolate box were some tiny crackers, made of shiny paper. Between them, Catherine and Anna lodged the crackers in the forks of the little tree's branches. Then they all gazed at the tree in silence, Catherine sitting back on her heels on the rug, Anna standing beside the table, Jennifer leaning forward from her armchair and Brenda sitting back in hers.

Catherine turned to her mother and said, 'Haven't we got a string of fairy lights?'

'I don't think we brought them with us,' Jennifer said.

'We did. They were in the box when you put it in the car. I saw them.' Catherine went out of the room and down the hall, to where many of the boxes they'd brought with them were still standing. She came back with a string of small, flower-shaped lights hanging between her hands, on green cable. She draped the lights over the gold and silver branches of the little tree, winding them round and round. They were a little too long, but not by much. The lights had lain unused for years in their box of decorations, always too short for their big tree.

Brenda bounced upright in her chair and said excitedly. 'There's a spare plug down behind the television.'

The lights had to be unwound from the little tree again, and then Catherine lay down on her belly to plug them in. They at once began to shine: red and green and blue. Jennifer brought the little tree and they stood it beside the television, on the cabinet. Catherine knelt up and draped the lights around the tree again, then jumped to her feet and darted across the room to switch off the light.

The little tree was the only patch of light in the darkness. Each of its small lights cast a mist of colour around it. The blue lights shone on the silver tinsel: the red lights shone on the gold. Bright points of light and a gleam of colour touched each little glass bauble. The light reached out and glinted on the globes hanging on the larger tree, which was all but hidden in the darkness.

'Ooooh!' Anna said approvingly.

'Oh, that's so pretty,' Brenda said again. 'You are clever, Catherine. Mother would have loved that. Your great-gran would have loved it.'

'Let's leave it up as long as ours,' Catherine said. 'Let's leave it up for Great-Gran.'

'Well, we ain't going to take it down now,' Jennifer said. 'Another drink, Mother?'

Brenda said yes, and Jennifer went into the kitchen and made hot chocolate for the children, and brought the bottle of wine back in with her. Brenda had turned on a small lamp, so that they could have enough light, and yet still enough darkness to appreciate the prettiness of the little tree.

As they drank their chocolate, Brenda told them about Christmas when she was a little girl. 'We had a real stocking –

I mean, we used one of our socks, not these big sacks you get now. We hadn't got much money. Our dad had died, see, so our mother – that's your great-gran–'

'The one who owned the little tree,' Anna said.

'That's right. Your great-gran had to go out to work, and her did work! But her always made sure we had an orange each in the toes of our socks, and some nuts and an apple – they was real treats when I was little, real treats – and a sugar mouse. We always had a sugar mouse for Christmas. The boys got white ones, and the girls had pink ones. And I had five brothers and sisters, remember, so it wasn't easy for your great-gran to find the money to buy all them apples and oranges and sugar mice. Have you got your stockings ready?'

'Great big sacks,' Jennifer said. 'They'm down the hall, waiting.'

Brenda leaned forward and tapped Anna on the nose. 'Ashes in your stocking if you ain't been good!'

'I've been good,' Anna said.

'I'll bet you haven't.'

'Father Christmas will bring me my presents anyway, won't he?' Anna said, and Jennifer told her, 'Of course he will, 'course he will.'

'You'd better leave a mince-pie and a glass of wine out for him, then,' Brenda said, and then Anna wanted to do that at once.

16

So they cleared away the old boxes that the Christmas decorations were kept in, and dusted the table clean of bits of old tinsel, and set out a little plate with a couple of mince-pies on it, and a glass of wine standing beside it. Catherine put some more pies on another plate, and poured another glass of wine and set them beside the little tree.

'Who's that for?' her grandmother asked. 'The reindeer?'

Catherine smiled, but didn't answer.

Soon after, she and Anna were sent off to bed. Their gran insisted on making them up hot-water bottles, even though the house was centrally heated and they didn't need them. Both women came upstairs to see the stockings – or sacks – hung on the doorknob of the bedroom Anna and Catherine were to share. It was all for Anna, really, who still believed in Father Christmas, but Catherine still enjoyed going through the ritual for Anna's sake. Their gran kissed them both, and then the women went back downstairs. Anna vowed that she was going to stay awake until Father Christmas came. She wanted to see him, but most of all she wanted to see the reindeer. She had an idea that they came into the house with him. Not down the chimney, of course, that would be silly. Through the door. But Anna was asleep within fifteen minutes.

Downstairs Brenda and Jennifer drank wine, and talked, pottered around getting small things ready, and put the turkey into the oven for the next day. Jennifer worked out how long

17

it would take to cook and set the oven-timer to cook it while they slept.

'I hope I've got enough in,' Brenda said. Her son and other daughter were coming the next day.

'Together with what I've brought, we've enough to feed the army, and put on a high-tea for the navy. Shall we go and be Father Christmas now?'

Giggling, the two women crept up the stairs. Catherine came quietly out of the bedroom to join them. Presents were fetched from the top of the wardrobe in Brenda's room, where they'd been stowed on arrival, while Brenda ferreted hers out of the various cupboards and drawers where she'd been hiding them for months. Every crackle and rustle of cellophane seemed likely to wake the neighbours, let alone Anna. When both Christmas sacks were bulky and bulging, they were returned to the landing outside the bedroom door, and Catherine went back to bed.

'I'm ready for my bed now,' Brenda said.

'Well, you go on and go to bed then, Mom. I can lock up.'

So Brenda went into the bathroom, while Jennifer went back downstairs. She collected cups and glasses from the living room and carried them out to the kitchen, where she checked again that she'd set the timer correctly. When the cups and glasses were washed up and put away, she made sure that the back door was locked, and went down the hall to lock the front door. She was about to go upstairs when she remembered the fairy lights on the little tree. Better turn them off. It wasn't likely that they'd cause a fire, but better safe than sorry.

As she pushed open the door of the living room she could see the faint glow of the coloured lights on the wall. The door swung further open, and Jennifer gave a wild start, backing into the hall, her hand rising to her throat. A figure, a stranger, sat in the armchair.

But not a stranger. Jennifer's hands dropped from her face as she recognised the head bent forward on the neck, the chin pulled up towards the nose, the stooped shoulders, the thin arms and hands folded in the lap.

The old woman sat in the armchair, staring towards the shimmering and sparkling, the coloured lights and shining baubles, of the little gold and silver tree.

The living room door swung back, until it almost closed, hiding the old woman from sight. Through the crack of the door left ajar came the faint glow of red, blue and green light.

Jennifer stood in the hallway. Slowly her hand rose, to reach out and push the door open again, but she withdrew it before it touched the painted wood.

She stood there some further minutes, and then went down the hall and turned off the light at the bottom of the stairs. The light on the landing was already off. She climbed the stairs by the dim grey light of a street-lamp shining through the glass panel in the front door.

Half way up, she stopped. Around the living room door shone the faintest haze of coloured light. The little Christmas tree was still shining. Perhaps it was still being admired.

Overheard In A Graveyard

What is Longing made of, that it never wears out?

Bone breaks. Rock wears away to sand. In this dark rain, hard iron falls to rust.

Razors blunt, but Longing's edge still cuts deep.

If you'd gone to another land, I could have followed, by road, by ship.

But no path will lead me to you, no door will let me through to you. There's no wall I can climb, no thorns I can fight through—

How can you be so far from me?

What is Longing made of, that there's more comfort in a bed of stone, a thorn pillow, sheets of ice?

Who weeps on my grave, who keeps me from sleep?

Is it you who unearths me to this cold rain, this dark, this wind and all this grief?

My bed was made; I lie in it. Hard frosts have cracked my bones. Down the rain has come and seeped me through. Twelve long months have passed and gone since I was warm and quick.

Go away, love.

Leave me to the grave.

I see you!

I can see you.

Can I touch you?

Let me hold you again. I never held any like I held you. There was never any touched me like you. Never since.

Can I rest my head on yours? Will you lay your head on my shoulder?

I want to hold you, warm—

I'm warm no more.

I'll warm you.

Ah, love. If I put my arms round you now, if I pressed me close to you now . . . Ah, love, your heart would catch and stop cold.

Go in from the rain now, and warm yourself.

In twelve months more you'll love some other – and love the more for losing me.

You store up grief, love – but never fear you'll miss your share of grief.

Get in from the wind, love.

Leave me to the grave.

Kiss me goodbye, then. One kiss.

My mouth is cold as the wet clay. My breath earthy strong. Go ask a kiss from a warmer mouth with sweeter breath than mine.

Go in from the cold, love.

Leave me to the grave.

I want to be with you.

Let me stay.

Is there room in that little house for me? Take me in out of the rain.

Let me hug you close – then there'll be room.

Let me in, please let me in. I'd sooner lie with you in that deep bed than stand under the sun and long for you.

There is no room.

Go from here now – you keep me from sleep!

Your every tear's a chain that holds me here; every sob a stone that weighs me down.

Have some thought of me! And turn your back and go, and leave me to the grave.

I think of you, always I think of you!

Forget, forget! Don't I try? I am hugging burning ice – wouldn't I loose it if I could?

What is grief made of, that it never blunts? A steel trap looses its jaws, but grief's a trap that won't loose me. If gnawing through my own wrist could set me free, I'd gnaw my hand off!

Let me in to you. Let me in out of the rain.

Is this love, to unearth me to this pain? Go from me, leave me, let me sleep.

I shall lie on your grave and howl your name. I shall weep dry earth to mud. I'll call and call your name until you come. Every night I'll howl you to me, every night, every night and all.

I never owned a thing but I shared it with you, never a thought, never a coin I had but I shared it with you – and now we'll share this grief, I swear, while the trap bites on me it shall bite on you.

Let me hold you. I was never held by any like you held me. I never held any since like I held you. Let me warm you, love.

Come to me, then, come here to me, love.

What? Now you draw back?

Don't you love me any more?

Cold –!

Hush now, hush, don't fear. Our bed's unaired, it's chill and damp – but it'll warm, it'll warm as I draw you in.

But so cold—

Beautiful

The escalators were still, frozen in uneven, ridged steps; but the fountain still worked, and the sound of its water-droplets rippling into its pool and pattering on the stone basin and floor was loud, now the music had been turned off. The sound of the fountain was a constant, night-long rain-fall; but no rain ever did fall inside the mall.

The bright, white disc of the moon moved in a black and grey sky, and shone down through the glass-roof into the third floor, and through the gallery on to the second floor, and through the gallery on to the ground floor; but even up on the third floor the grey light of the moon was lost amongst the flat, dim electric light. The electric light turned the windows of the empty shops into slabs of reflections; it made the endless stone-tiled floors of the mall look dusty; it hung grey shadows in the distances of the long corridors and floors.

Silence moved in the long halls. It followed noise. Derek's shoes clacked and scuffed on the stone tiles, and echoed from the walls and doorways; the wheels of his trolley squeaked and creaked, and drew echoes from the roof of the gallery above –

and after all these noises, silence followed, moving out of the corridors that opened from either side, moving down the staircases and frozen escalators from the floor above. Silence seemed to peer over the balconies at him. It stood beside him, so that he turned to look.

It wasn't a place built for silence or emptiness. It was a place meant to be crowded and loud, every one of so many, many shops, on three levels, all lit up and jostling with crowds, every one playing a different tape, drowning out the fountain. At night, abandoned, it held no peace.

Every night Derek checked into the mall-office, and then went into the complex through a staff-entrance, into a corridor of exposed breeze-blocks, steel piping and rust-stains streaked down the walls. He collected his trolley from a cupboard and pushed it through a pair of double-swing doors – into a huge place, vaster than any cathedral, a place of dimmed lighting, patterned stone tiles, marbled walls and pillars, fountains and stilled escalators, mirrors and plate-glass, sculptures and gardens. He pushed his machine through it all, to reach the further end where he would begin work. Beside him his reflection moved among the layers of reflections in the windows. Above him the silence peered down through the galleries, and behind him the silence followed.

He rarely saw anyone else while he worked – occasionally a security guard, or a supervisor. Other cleaners worked on other floors, but they started and finished at different times and had no reason to get together. They simply wanted to do their job, and then go home.

Derek would have spent the whole night in the mall, if allowed. It wasn't that he liked the work, but he didn't dislike it, and the spacious, glitzy surroundings of the mall were better than his flat. The wages weren't much, but enough to get the DSS off his back. Having the job meant that every evening he had a reason to leave his flat and catch a bus, which meant seeing people at the bus-stop and maybe having a bit of a talk with them. He could always get in some kind of remark to the bus-driver.

Then there would be a bit of talk in the mall-office, and, after the job was done, another chat, and a long walk home to his bed. It broke up his time, and justified his spending most of the day sleeping, and the rest watching television. He liked chat-shows.

They told him in the mall-office that they had trouble keeping cleaners, because people didn't like the loneliness. Derek didn't like the silence, or the gloom of the side-turnings he had to pass, but he was used to loneliness. He didn't mind working while other people were in the pub. He knew that if he was in the pub with them, they wouldn't take any notice of him. Before he'd got the cleaning-job, saying, 'Gimme a *Mirror*,' to a newsagent was often all he said to anyone in a day.

Once he'd reached the furthest end of his floor, he began work. First he emptied the rubbish bins into black plastic sacks, dragging the sacks with him as he went back towards the staff entrance. He fished drink cans and banana skins out of the fountain, picked orange peel and crisp packets out of the flower-beds. The windows of the shops on either side reflected the windows of the shops on the other side, and the flower-beds in between – and there was Derek's reflection swimming among all the others, superimposed on the real things that could be glimpsed through the glass. The plastic bags scratched and whispered on the tiled floors.

Once he'd taken the rubbish out to the skips, he returned the whole length of his floor, his footsteps loud, his reflection whirling from darkened window to window. Sometimes a dummy would seem to loom at him through a mist of reflections, and he would take it for real movement, a real person, and his heart would jump. Three floors above him, through the glass roof, he could see a little of the moon, hazily brilliant. He heard rain falling, but it wasn't rain. It was the fountain.

Reaching his trolley again, he began washing the floor. The bucket clanked every time he touched it, the mop swashed and splatted, and every noise was too loud, reaching far down the empty corridors and disturbing the silence which came out to investigate. When he'd first started in the job, he'd stopped work every few minutes, to listen for some alarming sound that he thought he'd heard through the noise he was making himself. He didn't do that so often now, but he was always keeping watch around him as he worked, peering into the doorways he passed, trying to see into stores through the haze of reflections, taking a good look down side corridors. He couldn't stand his own noise, and the nerviness it produced, for long at a time. When he reached the Garden Cafe, he always stopped for a break.

The Cafe had been set up at a junction of several corridors. Part of it was housed in an ornate summer-house of twisted ironwork, painted white, despite the fact that it was inside the mall and didn't need any protection from the weather at all. The round white metal tables, and the white chairs with their curved backs, were supposed to look elegant. Under the mixture of moonlight and dimmed electric light, they looked grey and lost, as if someone had dumped them there and gone away.

A grove of trees spread their branches over the tables, shadowing them with their leaves. The trees were all artificial, as were most of the bright flowers in the urns. Excellent imitations. You had to finger the leaves and petals before you could be certain that they weren't real. But somehow, once you knew they weren't real, you couldn't appreciate the look of them as much. From either side of the Cafe, rising up through the artificial trees, were two escalators. One was still switched off. The other had been turned on again, probably by the supervisor as he went on his rounds. It moved endlessly down and down with a low trundling sound.

Derek seated himself at one of the grey tables, under one of the artificial trees, and spread his meal out in front of him. A can of beer. A meat pasty, its paper bag serving as a plate. A bag of crisps. A bar of chocolate. He began with the crisps, and listened to the crackling of the bag push out into the silence, out of the circle of deserted tables into the dim corridors beyond. Something caught his eye and, looking up, he saw a single figure come into view on the slowly descending escalator, its head turning towards him.

Derek sat up straight. Not a security guard: no uniform. A supervisor, come to check up on him? Or another cleaner, from another level. He sat straighter, scooping his food together and trying to hide it with his arm, because he was ashamed of it. Not a proper sort of meal, crisps, pasty, beer.

Not a supervisor, not dressed-up enough. Some new type then, coming to ask him something. He wished they'd ask somebody else. Saying a few words to a bus-driver, or a newsagent was all he was good at. In those situations a few words was all there was time for, and nobody expected anything much. He cringed inwardly when he saw that the approaching stranger was a youngster. It wasn't that he disliked young people, but so many of them were slim and good-looking, well-educated, had friends and things like that. They embarrassed him.

The stranger reached the bottom of the escalator, and came towards him. A tall figure with long, straight dark hair swaying about the face and neck. A long baggy sweater, white and cable-knit, swung emptily from the shoulders to the knees. Beneath the sweater were jeans faded almost to whiteness, and trainers that made no more than a soft padding on the tiles of the mall.

The stranger came straight to Derek's table, and sat on the chair next to him. Derek kept his eyes on the table-top, and took another drink from his can of beer. He stared across the open space of the mall towards the dark windows of a store, where the white tables were reflected foggily. His spine stiffened, and his jaw set as he waited for the stranger to speak.

Come on, he thought. What do you want? The way to the office? The bogs? A fag? What?

There was no movement or sound from the stranger. The escalator went on trundling down and down.

With annoyance, even defiance, Derek turned his head and looked into the stranger's face – then quickly looked away again, feeling still more uncomfortable.

The stranger's hair fell straight to the shoulders, where it made a soft, heavy fold. Its dark brown shone the blond of

31

light wood where the mall's dimmed light struck it. Between these heavy falls of hair, the face was serious as it studied him – but a sweet seriousness, without any trace of severity. Large, grey eyes stared from beneath straight, heavy brows. A line of light traced the plane of the cheek from the corner of the eye to the corner of the mouth, and a fine dusting of gold down emphasised the moulding of the upper lip. The mouth was full, both upper and lower lips so curved that Derek's first thought was that they were puckering for a kiss. He quickly looked back at the table-top and his half-eaten pasty.

Beauty, to Derek, was embarrassing and disconcerting. However much he might admire it, he knew it had no use for him, so what was the use of it *to* him? His hand clenched on the beer can, and he concentrated on staring at the store windows across the way. This person would go, eventually. If he stuck it out, this person would go.

He flinched as the stranger beside him moved, but held himself back from any larger movement which might betray nervousness or fear. Instead he sat back a little in his chair and turned his head fractionally.

The stranger had merely leaned forward a little, and was looking enquiringly, but with great solemnity, into Derek's face. A mass of hair, having fallen forward, was still stirring gently, each strand so fine. The full lips still seemed to be in the act of puckering for a kiss. Now that they were closer,

Derek could see that the circles of grey in the eyes were ringed with a darker grey, and grained with violet and lavender. The intense black pupils at their centres were highlighted with shining points of white light.

Derek had been lifting his can of beer to his mouth and had paused, without realising it, while he stared at the colours in the eyes. Now he set the can sharply on the table and said, 'Well? What?'

The stranger leaned still further forward, the neck stretching out, the head tilting sideways, so that the hair fell sideways, at first lock by lock, but then in a rush. Some of it fell across the face, obscuring the intent grey stare and the puckering mouth.

Derek moved backwards, more embarrassed than alarmed – nothing about the stranger was threatening. The stranger pursued and, when Derek's back was pressed against his chair, and he was ashamed to move any further, the stranger's mouth touched against his.

It was a mere movement of the lips on his, with the faintest of sounds. He felt the long hair drift against his face, a brush of thistledown. Strands of the hair were trapped between their two mouths, were pressed, sharp and grainy, against the skin of his lips. Cold and dry as it was, the kiss tightened Derek's breath and made his heart thump and rattle. A joke, he thought, staring at the half-eaten pasty lying on its paper bag, surrounded by crumbs; at the opened beer can, the still wrapped chocolate bar. A joke, a joke. People will come down from the gallery above in a minute, laughing.

He didn't look round until he felt his hand touched, lifted. The stranger had taken his hand, was holding it, stroking it. The stranger's hands were as big as his, but younger and smoother. Derek's hand tensed within the stranger's hold, but though he felt anger, he didn't pull his hand away. It was pleasant, the stranger's touch, warm and smooth. Angry, yes, he was angry, because he was being mocked; but there was time to be angry yet.

The stranger lifted Derek's hand and kissed the big, rough-skinned knuckles. The touch of the lips was cool, soft, and dry. Above Derek's hand the stranger's large grey eyes stared at him from under the straight brows that gave them such a serious look. Serious, not mocking. There was no mockery in the face that watched him.

Because Derek didn't withdraw, the stranger, still watching him, turned his hand over and kissed the inner side of his wrist. As Derek watched, bewildered, fascinated, the stranger's head turned a little aside, and the lids closed over the grey eyes, laying long brown lashes on the cheek. Derek allowed his hand to stay within the stranger's hold, the stranger's lips pressed to his wrist. He waited.

Then the stranger's eyes opened again, a quick lift of the lids, revealing the eyes brightly turned to him, above his own hand. He could still feel the shape of the lips pressed against his wrist. The flash of the opening eyes – sudden, wary, even guilty – warned him. His whole arm tensed, and his hand moved a very little in the stranger's hold. But then he relaxed. He thought, quite clearly and coolly: What the hell.

As he relaxed, as if that was a signal, the stranger bit.

Derek felt the hard teeth press against the bones of his wrist, and pinch up the flesh – and then the piercing, which passed quickly from a pressure to a stinging and then barely tolerable pain. His arm jerked again, as he tried to snatch back his hand, but it was too late. The stranger held his hand tight.

Derek clenched his free hand into a fist and raised it high, with some idea of bringing it down on the stranger's head – but after holding the fist in the air for a moment, he brought it down on the table with a clang. His jaw cracked as he opened his mouth wide, gasping for breath. His heart fluttered. Relax, relax, he said to himself. There was a dragging at his wrist which spread into his arm. He could feel the veins of his arm being drawn, could feel his flesh whitening and drying. Another, smaller heart seemed to beat in his armpit. But the pain faded—

—or he got used to it. There was even something curiously pleasant about feeling the blood leave him. His face grew hot, his heart racketed and his chest felt tight – but he was drowsy too, drowsy and warm. The fact that his heart was racing didn't matter. Nothing much mattered. He had thought so for years, and now he knew it.

He looked at the stranger hunched over his hand – all he could see was a mop of brown hair that hid face and shoulders – and he thought: poor, hungry thing. He tried, with the thumb of his hand that was being bitten, to stroke the stranger's cheek, but wasn't successful. It moved his flesh on the teeth, and hurt; and the stranger clutched the harder at his hand.

'All right, okay,' Derek said, almost fondly, and let the feeding go on uninterrupted. He even lifted his can of beer and took another drink.

The stranger's teeth were withdrawn, and Derek's arm was neatly, politely replaced on the table, as if it was something inanimate that had to be put back where it belonged. When Derek turned his head, he met the gaze of the sweetly serious grey eyes while beneath their wide stare, the mouth worked. The full lips folded in on themselves. Behind them, the movement of the tongue could be seen, searching round the teeth. The tongue came out, red, to lick the lips. The throat swallowed.

Derek watched. 'Better?' he said, and laughed to himself.

The stranger rose and, in doing so, stooped and kissed Derek again, high on his cheek, near his eye. Then, with a swing of long hair and long, baggy jumper, the stranger moved away. Derek turned and thought he caught a glimpse of a tall figure moving into the dimness of one of the long corridors. There was a flash, a flicker in the darkened plate glass which might have been reflections of a long, pale jumper. But he couldn't be certain.

He finished his beer before he had the courage to examine his wrist. The wound was smaller than he had expected, though unpleasantly ragged and torn. It still bled, in a slow and watery way. The edges of the wound were white. Even the red flesh within seemed pale. 'Best put a plaster on that,' he said to himself: but as he had no plasters with him, it would have to wait. He rolled the sleeves of his shirt and jumper up, so the cuffs wouldn't catch on the edges of the wound.

He took his time over finishing his meal, and particularly enjoyed the chocolate, letting it melt in his mouth and working it into a paste with his tongue. Then he got up and finished his work, going slowly because he felt shaky. He had to go carefully because he found that he wasn't quite in control of his hands and feet. When he moved them, he couldn't be certain of where they would land. He didn't know if that was the result of blood-loss or simple shock.

After he'd put his equipment away, he signed off in the office. He didn't say anything about his visitor. Security wasn't his job.

It was a long walk home. He had to keep sitting down on

garden walls, feeling whoozy. As soon as he got in, he put a plaster on his wrist, although it had stopped bleeding. Not having to see the wound made him feel better. Then he had a cup of tea and went to bed, where he lay for a long time, thinking about the stranger.

The stranger didn't visit him again for a month. Every night for the first fortnight he went to work hopefully, and was on the watch as he went about the mall. He lingered at the Garden Cafe, giving it just another five minutes more . . . Nothing disturbed him except, occasionally, the sound of someone else working in one of the galleries above.

At the end of each night, disappointed, he went home, went to bed, and tried to remember what the stranger had looked like. In the afternoon he got up, watched the television, perhaps went to the corner shop, where he might say a few words about the weather or the latest scandal in the papers, but never, never anything about the stranger. It amused him to walk away from the shop, keeping to himself a story more remarkable than anything in that day's news. *I know something you don't know.* He would go home, have something to eat, watch more television, and go to work. Where he hoped to see the stranger, but didn't.

In the third week he began to lose hope of ever seeing the stranger again. He knew he hadn't dreamed or hallucinated the visit because why should he? – and anyway, the plaster still covered the healing bite on his wrist. Who else, he wondered, did the stranger visit? That made him angry. Why not *me*? Wasn't I good enough? I'm fat, I'm ugly, I'm a bore, I'm a loser, I'm a nothing – but I'm chock-full of blood and blood's blood, isn't it, for God's sake.

He wasn't even sure what the stranger looked like any more. He remembered the brown hair, that there was a lot of it . . . He remembered that the eyes had been large and grey – or, light-coloured, anyway. He remembered that the lips had been full – but these were words, mental notes. He could no longer make them into anything but the vaguest of pictures.

He was walking backwards, mopping the last stretch of floor before the Garden Cafe, when he looked over his shoulder, and there was the stranger, sitting on the wall of one of the raised flower-beds, amongst a mass of artificial flowers. This was a little more than a month after the first visit.

Derek stopped and turned round. His visitor rose from the wall and stood looking at him. Derek looked a long time, matching his uncertain memories to the real thing. There was the long, straight hair, springing from the centre of the forehead and falling in two wings, brown in the shadows, blond in the light. He had forgotten how straight and heavy the dark brows were, and the solemnity of the stare – so solemn, so wide-eyed and serious that it made him want to laugh. He'd forgotten the way the mouth seemed always about to kiss (because it was pushed forward by the teeth behind it?).

Derek went close and tapped his own mouth with his forefinger. 'Put one right there, Beautiful.'

Obediently, Beautiful leaned forward, and Derek brought up his hand to cup the back of his visitor's head. He almost started as he touched the long hair, its thickness and softness was so unexpectedly real after all his imagining. Cool, and so sleek that his hand moved over it as over ice.

He had expected the other to start back at his touch, but there was no withdrawal. He was allowed to urge their mouths together with his hand at the back of the other's head, and to press until the lips parted in a soft, wet kiss. Only when he pushed his tongue forward did the other pull away (because of the teeth those full lips must hide?).

Derek let go, but caught a lock of hair, and let it be drawn through his fingers as the other moved back. Already the other's head was tilting sidelong, the grey eyes moving down to Derek's hand, then lifting to look Derek in the face.

Derek was already raising his hand. 'I come cheap, don't I? Easy touch, that's me.' He offered his barely healed wrist. At least he'd taken the plaster off it. He watched as his visitor took hold of his hand and arm, raised his wrist as one might raise a corn-cob, and bit at it.

He was prepared for the pain this time and rode it, setting his teeth and hissing through them. When it had settled to the oddly pleasurable discomfort of feeling his veins drawn thin like wires, he lifted his other hand and gently moved the long hair that had fallen forward over his visitor's face, so that he could watch as the mouth worked and the cheeks hollowed. The eyes were closed, but a frown line appeared, and vanished, and appeared, again and again, between the brows. Watching, Derek wanted to touch the little frown-crease, smooth it away, but he was afraid that to go so far would frighten away his guest. Yes, his guest. Derek felt a tenderness, and a warm sense of his own kindness, as he had sometimes felt when feeding a stray cat a bowl of milk. He continued to stroke the long hair, gathering it up in cool, heavy handfuls, which slipped away through his fingers almost like water, and he would take another handful, to feel the sensation again. Sometimes the hair seemed too soft to feel. And only when he slipped his hand beneath the mass of hair did it seem even faintly warm.

'You go on,' he murmured, stroking his hand down the length of the hair. 'You have all you want. Drink up.'

But his visitor withdrew, straightening, gently releasing his arm, gently withdrawing out of his reach, though a skein of hair still trailed from Derek's hand and fanned out into a fine, shining web. Again Derek watched the full mouth working, removing the last of his blood from the lips and teeth, and swallowing it, while the grey eyes stared solemnly at him.

Derek cradled his bitten hand in the palm of the other. He

felt a little dizzy. The long empty corridors of the mall seemed to stretch away from him even further than usual: their dimness was spangled, their silence hummed. The colours of the artificial flowers and trees, the bright blocks of chairs, seemed more vivid than usual, even in the half-light. His mouth was dry and his throat sore with thirst. 'I hope you'll come back a bit sooner next time,' he said. 'Don't be such a stranger.'

His visitor took a step backwards, and gave a smile so slight that the mouth hardly moved, though the cheek dimpled slightly. It was a shy smile, that seemed afraid of giving offence, and it charmed Derek. 'You don't have to run off,' he said. 'Stop a bit. I'm going to have me dinner. Stop and keep me company.' His visitor continued to back away, step by step. Derek followed. 'Where you going, any road? C'mere.' He let go of his bitten hand, though it ached, and reached out to catch the arm of his visitor.

The other, instead of dodging, stopped moving and stood absolutely still. And Derek, in the act of reaching for his visitor's arm, took the message of that stillness and backed away instead.

The visitor turned and ran, vanishing almost immediately around the block of the escalators. The sound of light, running footsteps came drifting back to Derek for some seconds, travelling well in the silence of the empty mall.

Derek went back to the Cafe, nursing his bitten hand, and

sat. He felt hot and sick, and it was a while before he got up and fetched his meal from his trolley. The beer was good, moistening his sorely dry throat. Where are you going? he'd asked his visitor. As if he didn't know. As if it took a lot of figuring out.

He chomped his way through a cold beef and onion pie, and drank beer, thinking of all the night-places. The half-darkened supermarkets where one or two people wander around the fixtures, stacking the shelves. The all-night chemists with the counters covered in white sheets and all but one aisle of lights turned out. The nurses sitting in darkened wards full of sleeping patients: the ambulance stations, the night-shifts at fire-stations. The watchmen patrolling silent corridors or sitting by the light of one lamp listening to a tinny radio that will fall silent at four. The long streets of doorways, the subways and the graveyards where the dossers slept. The taxi-ranks where drivers waited and waited, half-hoping and half-afraid that a fare would turn up. All, like him, lonely people and among them, like him, the more than lonely; the ones who had given up hope of ever being anything but lonely.

And his Beautiful going from one to another. Perhaps staying longer with some than with others. Perhaps paying some with more than a small, cool kiss. Why did he get only a small kiss? He was giving *blood*, for God's sake.

He had hugged to himself the idea that he knew something

43

amazing that had never been broadcast on television, or printed in a newspaper. He had walked out of the newsagents, and grinned to himself on the pavement, thinking of what he knew. But now he saw that hundreds of people must know his secret, and he felt the anger that every fool feels when he finds that he's been short-changed. He imagined some grubby dosser or spotty shelf-filler being allowed to touch Beautiful's hair as he had done, and his anger turned sick. Then he thought: This must be jealousy! He was surprised to find himself feeling jealousy, as might any normal man who had friends and lovers. He ended by being grateful to Beautiful for making him feel jealous.

He bought liver, and a big bottle of expensive vitamin tablets with added iron, because he'd picked up from somewhere – from some chat-show or newspaper article – that liver, and iron and vitamins were good for the blood. Made it stronger. He hated the liver, but he fried it and ate it every day. For Beautiful, he told himself as he forked it into his mouth. If he let his blood get all thin and watery, Beautiful would go elsewhere.

Some days he didn't feel good. He got tired easily and out of breath, but he never missed a night at work. The mall was the only place Beautiful knew where to look for him. He wouldn't risk missing Beautiful.

But the nights went by and went by, and his only visitors

were security guards and supervisors, who complained about how slow he was. But he didn't hurry because the longer he took, the longer Beautiful had to find him. He wasn't worried about getting the sack: well, no more worried than everybody was these days. Easy enough to get another cleaner, yes, but they didn't stick with the job like he did. And if he did his work slowly, he did it thoroughly.

The long, quiet nights gave him plenty of time to think about Beautiful, and where Beautiful was, and what other people got in exchange for their blood. Often, when he was angriest, his anger would suddenly collapse and give way to depths of tenderness as he remembered stroking Beautiful's hair, and thought of that so serious look, that had something of pleading in it. Poor thing: always so hungry. In that mood he felt he wanted nothing but to be allowed to feed Beautiful full, and hold Beautiful and stroke the long hair. He'd been lonely all his life. Now he had this, and it was strange and it was special. Why be greedy?

If he could just know where Beautiful was, and that Beautiful was safe: that was all he wanted. To shut Beautiful up in the box of his flat, to lock the door. He'd keep the secret; he'd tell no one, boast to no one. Safe. Beautiful wouldn't have to go wandering out in the cold and rain any more. With him, Beautiful would be safe. He liked those words.

But it would nag away at the back of his mind until he had

to admit it – he couldn't feed Beautiful for even one night. Face it, Beautiful had gone straight from him to some other mug each time. It made his breath come short, and his heart tight. Did any memory of him ever cross Beautiful's mind, once his blood had been swallowed? Or was there only a vague connection between this place in the mall and food, as there must be a connection in the brain of a stray cat between a particular place and meat?

Kill it, that was what he should do. Wouldn't be murder. How could you murder a thing like that? Who would miss it? – Well, he would, and God knew how many like him who would wait, and wait, and be sad because Beautiful didn't come in the night any more. But who would *report* it missing? No one, and that was what counted. And all those others who would miss Beautiful, well, that just served them right.

He planned the killing for a night or two, even started to take a knife into work with him, one long enough, he thought, to stab to the heart. But then, as the long nights continued to pass without any sign of Beautiful, he grew sad and his mood swung round again. What did he care how many people fed Beautiful, so long as Beautiful came to him as well? So long as he was allowed to stroke the long hair for a few minutes, what did he care? He'd work at being grateful for what he had.

He put the knife back in the kitchen drawer, but when he had counted out more than a month, night by slow night, and sickened with disappointment, he took it out again, and put it back in his pocket.

It was in his pocket as he mopped the last few feet of floor before the Garden Cafe and his break. The feeling that he had a silent follower, more persistent than usual, made him turn suddenly. He jumped to find Beautiful pacing beside him, head a little stooped to look at him, long hair swinging, smiling that slight, shy smile as if unsure of welcome.

Derek stood his mop in its bucket. For a second the silence was absolute: then the pattering of the fountain was heard. Turning, Derek held his arms wide. Beautiful stepped back, as if to avoid the embrace, but then allowed it. Derek wrapped his arms tightly around the other's body and felt it sway towards him and lean heavily on him. 'Aaaaah,' he said, and patted the other's back, revelling in how slight the body was, how easy to hold, how light to support. He felt tenderness and pity. As if there would be no welcome! He reached up and smoothed the long hair away from Beautiful's face, gleeful because he was allowed to do that. He combed the hair with his fingers, smoothed the straight brows and gently closed the eyes with his thumbs, gently tilted down the head and kissed the mouth. Beautiful would not stop him, would not draw back, until after the feed. 'Long time, no see,' he said. 'I missed you, y'know.'

He took Beautiful's hand, which was cold. Well, it was cold out. 'You'm going to stop with me a bit tonight. Come on.

Come and sit with me while I have me dinner.' He took his dinner from the cleaning trolley and led Beautiful, by the hand, to the white summer-house in its arbour of artificial trees and flowers.

At the table, Derek set out his can of beer, his bag of crisps, his bar of chocolate, and took his pasty out of its bag, laying it on top of the paper. 'Same old junk,' he said. 'Same old rubbish I stuff down me neck every night. Want some? Help yourself – half the pasty. Have the chocolate, just have it. – Don't you eat anything at all? I s'pose not. Stupid question. Wouldn't need to come to me if you did, would you?'

He broke off the end of the pasty and put it into his mouth. 'You don't have to stop away so long, y'know. You could come every night for me, and welcome. You could. I'd be glad to see you. Don't worry about me. I got plenty in me. 'Cos of being fat, see. That's one good thing about being fat: you've got plenty of blood. Sa fact, that is. And I been building it up, eating liver and that. So you could come tomorrow, and the night after, and every night.'

The sound of his voice seemed to make an enclosure around them: his words so loud under the papery leaves of the Cafe's trees, louder even than the fountain's pattering. Yet such a short distance from them was an expanse of silence, reaching away into the corridors, and up to the galleries above. Beautiful sat listening, head on one side and a fall of long hair shining in the mall's half-light. No flicker of understanding crossed Beautiful's face. *Does it understand?* Derek wondered. *Has it ever understood a word I've said?*

Reaching out, Derek took Beautiful's hand and played with it, turning it over in his own, stroking the smooth skin with his thumb. It gave him great happiness, both the sensation, and the fact that he was allowed to do it. With his free hand, he continued to eat his pasty and drink from his can of beer. Beautiful began to lean forward, towards Derek's hand.

'Ah-ah!' Derek said warningly, and took his own hand away. *Now there's a thing,* he thought. *I'm the one to pull back.* He felt oddly proud. 'Not so easy tonight, Beaut. You'm going to have to sing for your supper tonight. What's your name, any road?'

He hadn't expected an answer, and got none. He put the last of his pasty into his mouth and, rising from his chair, stood above Beautiful, who looked up at him. Derek pushed his hand into the other's long hair, and lifted the hair, feeling the weight of it, and let it fall. He perched himself on the edge of the table and played with the hair, as if it was in itself something important to do, twisting a strand around his finger, brushing it across the face that looked up at him, making the grey eyes blink. He gathered all the hair up together and let it fall, feeling it wash around his hand like soft water.

'Where d'you go?' Derek asked. 'I mean, when you go from

here, and in the day? What do you do?' His hand was cupped at the side of Beautiful's head, buried in the long hair. Beautiful's head turned, and the mouth opened at his wrist. 'Oh no.' Derek withdrew his hand from the fullness of hair, setting it swinging and resettling lightly. Derek withdrew to the other side of the table, and grinned. 'Boot's on the other foot tonight, petal, int it?' He opened his bag of crisps and settled back in his chair. He ate crisps as he watched Beautiful lean towards him over the table. He watched the full lips purse and then part as the intent gaze fixed, not on his face, but on his hand.

'What it is to be wanted,' Derek said, and laughed. 'Sure you don't fancy a crisp?'

Beautiful seemed to relax, leaning back and looking about the emptiness of the mall, at the shop doorways, the window displays, the elaborately lettered signs.

Thinking of leaving, Derek thought. He said, 'You don't want to keep wandering about, up and down all night. You want one place to stop.' The words got harder to speak as he came closer to what he wanted to say. 'Somewhere . . . safe. Somewhere you'd be safe. Where you'd got – got . . . Got somebody to look out for you.' He cleared his throat and then, bravely, looked straight at Beautiful and said, 'Somebody to look after you.' The words 'to look after you' were lovely to him, like poetry. Tears rose to his eyes as he spoke them. He took a deep breath and said, failing to sound casual. 'You could stop with me if you like.'

Beautiful rose, came round the table with a swing of the long, shapeless jumper, and sat on a chair close beside Derek, so close that Beautiful's hair, swinging forward, brushed the arm of his sweater and left a brown hair behind. Derek was taken aback. Was this acceptance of his offer? But he saw from the other's face that Beautiful hadn't understood – or, at least, hadn't heard – a word. Beautiful had something else in mind; and looked into Derek's face with that serious, pleading and very sweet look.

In response, Derek reached out his hand to touch the other's cheek and move aside the hair. Beautiful's head turned with the movement of his hand, the mouth opening as it neared his wrist. Derek withdrew his hand sharply. For the first time – oddly, it *was* the first time – he felt afraid of Beautiful. Not just surprised, or wary, or nervous, but truly afraid. Yet nothing about Beautiful was threatening – except. Except for a stillness, an intentness. I always gave before, Derek thought. This is the first time I've held back . . .

He pushed his chair back, and its legs screeched across the tiles with a noise that echoed from the underside of the gallery above, and from the surrounding walls. Anyway, I've got the knife in my pocket, he thought. Thank God I've got the knife in me pocket. He reached into his pocket, feeling for the knife's handle, and looked for the spot on the white sweater where he would have to shove it. He clenched his hand around the wooden handle, and felt the muscles jump in his arm as he rehearsed the blow in his mind.

He got to his feet, not really knowing why, except that he felt safer on his feet. Beautiful rose too. Derek began to move, slowly, back towards his original seat, where his bar of chocolate still lay. Beautiful followed, the long hair stirring about the shoulders with every step.

Derek walked round the table and chairs, so that the clutter of furniture was an obstacle between them. He picked up the chocolate bar, unwrapped it and wagged it like a teacher's pointer. 'Think about it. You'd be better off with me to look after you.' He liked saying that. 'I'd look after you well. I could make the place dark, if that's what you need. Black the windows out. Easy. Anything you like. I'd look after you really well.'

Beautiful came close to the table and leaned far across it, hands landing on the metal surface with a thump. Staring at Derek across the short distance between them, Beautiful's mouth opened and let out an odd noise, a sort of whine. It reminded Derek of a dog's whining, warning growl.

'All right,' he said. He was being cruel, and why? He moved around the table and, sitting on its edge, offered his wrist, his left wrist, to Beautiful, who seized it and bit so fast and hard that Derek hardly had time to register the pain before it was over, and had changed to the drawing, pulling sensation that reached deep and far along his veins, and was oddly peaceful. He dropped his chocolate on to the table, so that he could stroke and pet Beautiful's lowered head. 'That's better, int it?' he said. 'Why was old Dekker being nasty, eh? Nasty old Dekker: never mind him. You have all you want.' But then, he thought, Beautiful would go away again, for another long month. That was no good.

It was hard to rouse himself to do anything about it, because the blood loss made his heart-beat echo in his ears, flushed his face, and made him drowsy. But if he didn't act, Beautiful would quickly finish feeding, and then go away even quicker.

So he shook his head, dragged in a breath, sank his hand into Beautiful's long hair and wrapped it around his fingers. He began to drag the head up and back and, at the same time, to pull his wrist away from the mouth, fighting against the grip of Beautiful's fingers. It hurt, and it wasn't easy, but Derek was determined and yanked at his handful of hair. Beautiful's head twisted back, the mouth open wide and he saw the teeth for the first time. They came forward to make the bite easier, so producing that beautiful pout, and they were long. Blood and slaver hung from them to the lips in viscous strings. My God, thought Derek: oh my God.

Beautiful gave a choking gasp and rolled desperate eyes, white-edged, animal eyes, but Derek continued to drag on the long hair, while twisting his bitten hand free. Then he darted several feet away. The knife! he thought, and felt for it in his pocket.

Beautiful still stood by the table, frowning, and making those familiar movements of the mouth, sucking blood from the teeth and gums, licking it from the lips.

Derek felt sorry, even ashamed, as he saw the disordered hair and the frown that seemed puzzled. He felt as if he had thrown a stone at one of his stray cats.

Then Beautiful turned round and began to walk away. Derek's heart jumped, panic shot through him. 'No – no, don't go! I didn't mean you to go.' He hurried after and caught hold of the other by the arm. Beautiful immediately became still, rigid, but Derek took no notice. He began to tow Beautiful back towards the table. 'Don't be like that. I didn't mean you to go. I only wanted you to stop longer. I know you got no use for me – I only wanted to keep you a bit longer, just a bit longer.'

He brought Beautiful back to the table, where he propped himself again, and offered his hand. Beautiful looked into his face, seeming uncertain. Derek raised his still bleeding wrist to the mouth, pressed it against the lips. 'Go on. I won't plague you again. Go on, get it down you.'

Beautiful's mouth opened and bit again, though the grey eyes still turned and strained to look at Derek from their corners, as if still not trusting him. But as he stroked the hair, the eyes closed, and the cheeks hollowed as the mouth worked, drawing out Derek's blood.

But in a minute or so, Derek thought, as he filled his hand with soft hair and stroked the long back, maybe in less than a minute, I shall be on my own again. It'll be another month, or more before it's my turn again. He foresaw another long month of nights where he spent the day hoping to see Beautiful, and the night listening and looking for Beautiful, and finally walked home to bed, disappointed and sad. The long misery of it, concentrated into a few seconds of sensation, not thought, pierced him through.

And even if Beautiful came again, there would be a short hour of frustrated happiness, and then another long, dragging month . . . And so it would go on, and on . . .

There was only one way to end it. He let the handful of hair he held cascade through his fingers, and then reached into his pocket and took hold of the knife. He didn't want to do it, but if he didn't . . . It was no good being drowsy . . .

He felt the teeth leave his flesh with a fine, sharp, sliding pain. Beautiful's head began to lift, the mouth already working to clean the teeth.

Moving dreamily, but with a dream-like assurance, Derek took the knife from his pocket, slipped his arm around Beautiful's shoulders, and put the knife-blade to Beautiful's throat. Beautiful was pressed back against his shoulder, their cheeks were together. Once more he pressed his bitten, ragged, bleeding wrist to Beautiful's mouth. 'Finish it,' he said.

Beautiful moved within his arm, trying to move away. Derek, in a sort of fright in case he should fail, twisted the knife and jabbed its blade sharply into the flesh of Beautiful's neck. He heard the other give a choking gasp of alarm, and felt the body stiffen against his side. Their cheeks pressed more tightly, warmly together as Beautiful's head tried to turn. The long, soft hair was rubbed against his face.

'Go on,' Derek said, still offering his wrist. 'Drink it all. May as well. Save you the trouble of coming back for it. Go on why don'tcha?' He pushed his wrist hard against the mouth, pushing the head back against his arm, smearing the lips with blood.

The teeth went in again, and Derek sighed. He turned the knife-blade away from the throat, but left his arm slung around the other's shoulder, letting his hand ride the working of the throat muscles. 'Yeah, go on,' he said. 'Enjoy yourself. Have a good blow out. You're lovely. You're my lovely.'

He could feel the veins of his arm, and then the veins of his neck and chest. As the blood left him, his heart began to beat faster, and faster – and every faster beat meant that there was still less blood in him. His mouth gaped, as he gasped for breath. There was a noise in his ears, a roaring, as if he had huge shells pressed to them.

Yet there was no pain, and no fear. He felt warm, and the pain had withdrawn somewhere behind the warmth, the soft, woolly, cosy warmth. The sensations were there: the ever-quicker double-thumping of the heart in the ever-tighter chest, the yawning for breath, but the pain was all muffled and he felt, not afraid, but happy. As he felt himself sink, as he felt his own arm drag on Beautiful's shoulder, he rubbed his face against the cheek next to his, and turned his head and, nuzzling under the cape of hair, kissed the neck, kissed the ear.

And sank. And floated.

He floated near the mall floor. Beautiful knelt beside him, above him, licking bloodied lips, licking teeth, swallowing. Beautiful shone, was made of light, and was fading – shining hair, shining skin, shining eyes – fading into a spangled mist, not of darkness, but of light, of white.

Derek tried to speak, but had no breath, nor space for breath. He wanted to lift his hand, to catch hold of a strand of hair and pull Beautiful's head down, but he couldn't move his arm or lift his hand. He was still concentrating on the strand of hair he couldn't reach when Beautiful vanished into the white light.

Still he heard. He heard the pattering of the fountain, like rain falling. He heard his own last breath begin its strangled, rattling course in his throat. And he heard a curious sound: something that might have been a whine, or a moan. Then hearing stopped too.

The moonlight shone down through the glass roof of the upper gallery, mingled with flat, electric light, and went on down to the second floor, and so on to the ground floor, where it shone on the little white summer-house of the Garden Cafe, and spread blurred shadows of its ironwork over the tiles, and scattered shadows of the trees' artificial leaves.

The light bounced from window to window, casting reflections of reflections back and forth between the walls of dark glass, until the displays behind the glass were lost in a gauze of reflections. It shone flat on the patterned stone tiles, and on Derek, lying there, short and fat and grubby, gaping up at the moon three storeys above.

Caisho Burroughs

I

During the reign of the first Elizabeth, there came to London and the court a youth named Caisho Burroughs. He quickly became famed for his unusual, even extraordinary, beauty. His legs were long and well-shaped, his waist small, his shoulders wide, his hair thick and shining; and his face so striking, with such fine eyes, such a pleasing mouth and white teeth, that everyone, men and women, stared after him in amazement that such a vision should walk, eat, spit, curse and fart.

If the fame of his beauty were not enough, he was soon as well-known for his quickness to see offence in the least remark or gesture; and for his vengeful temper, difficult to soothe. He had not been in town a year before he had fought three duels, though duelling had been forbidden by Royal Order. With sword in one hand and dagger in the other, he wounded all three of his opponents, and came near to killing the third.

If the Queen was displeased, she was not more so than

Caisho's father, and Caisho was packed off to Italy, to the city of Florence. Old Burroughs told his friends that he intended his son to see something of the world, and learn to speak Italian, but it was plain to all that his purpose was to keep his lovely but discreditable son out of the town's gossip for a while.

Many who knew Caisho predicted that he would soon find his way into the gossip of Florence; and so it proved.

At that time the Duke of Florence kept, as his mistress, a certain buxom, beautiful and talented lady named Giovanna. Though no longer a girl, she was much younger than the Duke, and far from faithful to him. She was amusing herself by watching the people pass in the street below her window when she saw Caisho, with his pale English skin and his fair hair shining in the sun. So taken with him was Giovanna that she sent her maid running after him, to fetch him to her.

After that day, Caisho often visited the lady, in secret, and Giovanna grew greedy for him. As often as he came, she wished him to come again: even on days when the Duke also visited her. Many a time Giovanna's maid let Caisho out of the side door as the Duke was entering at the front – or let Caisho in as the Duke was leaving.

And yet Caisho gave the woman little enough reason to love him. With his beauty, the appeal of his foreignness, and the charm of manner he could use when he chose, he was soon run after by both women and men. 'There are many, many womens,' he told Giovanna, 'more pretty as you, and more younger—' and see, this one had given him a pearl brooch for his hat, and this one a sapphire drop for his ear . . .

So foolish was Giovanna in her love that she too made Caisho presents of money, and gifts of jewels and clothes. She ran through her allowance from the Duke, and would have been afraid to ask for more for herself – but was more afraid that Caisho would not visit her if she could not lure him with costly bait.

The Duke, when asked for more money, listened to her excuses of having spent too much on new dresses, hats and jewels, and believed none of them. He knew that she was not faithful to him, but had thought it beneath him to notice her affairs with bakers, gardeners and priests. She wasn't his wife, after all. But Giovanna had never made lavish gifts to her other lovers. Rather, it had been they who brought gifts to her. As did the Duke himself.

The Duke accordingly made enquiries among his acquaintance, and soon heard more than enough of the frequent visits to his mistress by the young Englishman, Caisho Burroughs. And more than enough of the gold coin and gold chain, the brooches and finger-rings, the point-laces and shoe-buckles, the silks and velvets and brocade which Giovanna had given him.

The Duke had heard gossip of Caisho, and had even seen

him when Caisho, as was courteous in a foreign visitor, had attended the Duke's court. The Duke had been struck, as was everyone, by the Englishman's beauty but, having no taste for young men himself, the Duke had not seen him since. Now, however, a certain ardour was lit within the Duke concerning Caisho, and he set spies to watch.

When the spies reported to the Duke that Caisho had entered his mistress' house only minutes after he had left it himself, he was affronted and furious. Seeing Caisho again, at court, his fury grew, for Caisho was taller than he; and the Duke was losing his hair and gaining a paunch. In short, the Duke fell as deep in jealous hatred of Caisho as Giovanna had fallen in love. But the Duke had a cure for his ill. He ordered Caisho's murder.

It was Caisho's good fortune that, among the Duke's friends was a man who loved Caisho, and had given him presents and done him many favours, though never receiving more in return than a smile, and thanks spoken in poor Italian. This man could not bear to think of Caisho's beauty spoiled by a knife, and thrown into the Arno as carrion. Risking his own life, this man warned Caisho of the Duke's intention, and even helped him to leave Florence. Caisho, smiling, thanked him in poor Italian, and then, being tired of Italy, made his best speed out of that country and into France. He travelled the faster for having left most of his luggage behind.

The Duke of Florence, when he discovered Caisho's escape, turned all his anger on Giovanna, raved at her and beat her, and told her that her cowardly lover had run away, caring more for his own hide than for her spoiled charms. She, in terror of the Duke, and despairing at the knowledge that Caisho had never loved her, and that she would never see him again, took a dagger and stabbed herself to death.

II

Caisho was ignorant of Giovanna's death, but nor did he stay on his journey to allow any news from Italy to catch him. Reaching the Channel, he took ship for England, then bought a horse and rode to London. On arriving, he was pleased to find his younger brother, John, staying in his lodgings. He immediately made his brother presents of a brooch, chain and thumb-ring which had been given him in Italy.

They went out together to dine and, at the eating-house, met old friends, who gathered to the brothers' table and drank to Caisho's return. Because they admired the costly and foreign jewels he wore, Caisho gave to one the sapphire drop from his ear, to another the pearl brooch from his hat, and to others rings and chains. He could not remember with any certainty who had given them to him. The only things he had from

Italy with which he would not part, no matter how they were admired, were a matching sword and dagger of the finest, deadliest manufacture. They had been given him by that same man who had helped him escape from Florence.

Long after dark, drunk and tired, the brothers returned home and, there being only one bed, they climbed into it and fell asleep side by side.

A woman's voice woke them, calling, 'Caisho!' Raising themselves, they both saw, standing at the bed's foot, a woman dressed in loose white robes. Against the darkness, and her long black hair that mingled with it, her face showed still whiter than her linen, and from within blue shadows her dark eyes stared and stared as if she could not move or close them. She stared at Caisho.

Her eyes held the brothers in silence and stillness. She fumbled at the neck of her shroud with blue-fingered hands and pulled it open. They saw her white breasts, disfigured with open wounds. Caisho, who had seen those breasts when they were warm and beautiful, trembled so hard that he shook the bed beneath them.

Through stiff jaws, with difficulty, the woman spoke, on a sigh, like the sigh that will often escape a corpse. She said: 'Cai-sho.'

That word only: and between one blink of the eye and the next, she was not there. Caisho fell back on the pillow. John jumped from the bed and ran to the spot where the woman had stood. Nothing was there but a cold that made him gasp.

The cold, and the darkness of the room, which still whispered with the apparition's sigh, set him shaking, and he scrambled back into the bed, where he pulled the covers over the heads of both himself and Caisho. Through the rest of the night he lay awake, shuddering, and clinging tight to Caisho's senseless body.

Bright morning came, and calmed the worst of John's fear. He even began to think he had dreamed the night's terror. But when Caisho woke, he had dreamed the same dream. From that day to the end of his short life, Caisho knew no peace.

Even in a friend's lodgings, he could not bear to have the door of a room stand open, because of what might slip through it behind his back. But nor could he bear a door to be shut, for fear of what might be standing, unseen, on the other side.

Many, many times he was seen to turn, with a start, to look behind him. His own mirror he threw away, and he could not abide a mirror anywhere he was, but would jump up and turn it to the wall, because of what he glimpsed reflected there.

John, anxious for his brother, made sure he was surrounded by friends, but the liveliest company brought Caisho no ease, for he was constantly counting the people present. No assurances, no lighting of more candles, nor even the shining of those candles into every dark corner, could rid Caisho of the notion that another had come in, unnoticed, and was standing or sitting among them.

Caisho feared even crowded streets in daylight, and walked with lowered head, fearing that, if he raised his eyes, it would be to look into her stare.

It was a week after the dead woman's first appearance that Caisho and John were at dinner among friends. Caisho had been silent, as he now always was, but broke through the talk with a loud and quavering cry. His alarmed friends, looking where he did, saw a woman standing in a shadowed corner, her long black hair melting into the darkness while her white face and shroud shone lividly, like the moon in a dark sky. She neither spoke nor moved, but stared on Caisho with a fixity until she vanished.

After that, the appearance of the ghost was foretold by the colour blanching from Caisho's face, leaving it grey and cold as clay. He would sweat, and shake with such violence he could neither stand nor even sit on bench or stool unless he was held by others. His teeth clashed. His eyes fixed themselves on some patch of empty air, and he cried out, 'She comes! Oh God, she comes, she comes!'

Visitors who feared to see the apparition would hurry to

leave, for next the dead woman, glaring, would appear where Caisho gazed.

Caisho's friends soon fell away, even those who had accepted from him pearls, sapphires and table-cut diamonds. With many, it was not fear of the ghost that made them stay away, but fear of Caisho. The haunting made him yet more tempersome, and he never left his rooms without belting on the Italian sword and dagger. He had even drawn on his brother John, though a moment later he had thrown his own arm across his eyes and turned away.

III

It happened that, as John and Caisho were one day making their way to an eating-house, almost a month after the ghost's first appearance, a stranger jostled against Caisho, and knocked him into the filth of a brook, soiling his boots. Though the man apologised, Caisho would not accept, but pushed the quarrel and pursued the man even with John hanging on his arm, and spoke with such contempt that the man at last could do nothing but agree to meet Caisho at first light in the open fields nearby.

It was John who lay awake that night while Caisho, exhausted, slept, though he woke suddenly before dawn. He started to dress for the duel, but his hands shook so he could not fasten buttons or tie strings, and John went to help him. 'Send word that you withdraw,' John begged. 'Fight not today: you are nowise fit for it.'

'Never,' Caisho said, and shuddered, and stared with fixed eyes at the corner behind John's shoulder. John hugged him tight, but couldn't contain the trembling: and trembled himself when the woman appeared, white face and white shroud, from the corner's darkness. She held out stiff arms. Staring from a white, stiff face, she made a kissing mouth with blue lips, and was slow in her fading.

They were late for the meeting, but John could not keep Caisho from it. The other man, when he saw Caisho's pale face and the tremors that still ran through him, thought him sick and offered to withdraw. But Caisho called him coward, and a nothing; a cock who crowed from a dunghill but had no belly for the fight; a craven, pigeon-hearted runagate. All the while he advanced on the man with his sword and dagger drawn, making passes with them until, between shame and anger, the man took up his own weapons.

Caisho's attack was fierce, and put his opponent in fear for his life as he desperately sought to block blows from both the sword and dagger. He lost many chances to strike a blow himself through fear that, in doing so, he would feel the point of the Italian sword or dagger enter him. But, growing desperate as he tired, he lunged – and nothing blocked his sword but Caisho's heart.

John ran to Caisho, and knelt over him, but Caisho, with fixed eyes, looked through him and beyond him. John, turning his head, cried, 'Oh God, she comes! She comes!'

But there was no woman in the duelling field. When John turned back to his brother, Caisho was dead, and his great beauty already in decay.

With apologies to John Aubrey, who first reported Caisho Burroughs' story, as true, in his 'MISCELLANY'. The above is loosely based on it, from memory.

Padfoot

I'll tell you a true story – how my dad met the ghost dog.

Padfoot haunts lonely roads and lanes, padding along in the dark. It's bad luck to meet him. It means you're going to die soon. Everybody knows that, even if they don't believe it.

My dad didn't believe in ghosts when he met Padfoot. He was a grown man at the time, married, with three children – me, my brother and my sister. Dad used to work all hours to earn enough to keep us. He'd often go to work before we got up, and come home long after we'd gone to bed.

The night he met Padfoot, he'd stayed at work late, to finish an urgent job. It was midnight before he was able to put out the workshop's lights, lock up and start the walk home.

Midnight, the very witching hour, when graves gape wide and give up their dead. It was a cold, cold January night, with a freezing fog that blanked out streets and turned the light from the street-lamps into grey darkness. Nobody was about, and Dad's footsteps clumped dully back to him from the walls. Fog does that: makes it so you can't see a thing, but every sound is loud and dull and close-by.

The last bus had gone, so Dad had to walk. He had a good two miles to go, probably nearer three, and even though he'd been working since six that morning, he stepped out brisk. He had his hands stuck in his pockets, but the cold was seeping through the soles of his boots into his toes, and the freezing fog was biting his ears and giving him a headache. My dad's bald, and he didn't have a hat.

But, apart from getting colder and more tired, nothing worth mentioning happened until he came to the bottom of Turners Hill Lane.

Now Turners Hill Lane was a country lane that had got left over in the middle of all the factories and houses of the Black Country. It was really steep, and there were no buildings along it at all – nothing but hedgerows. It didn't even have pavements or street-lights. There was a lamp-post at either end of the lane, but none in between. So, once you turned into Turners Hill Lane, you'd not only got a hard climb in front of you, but a lonely, dark one too.

An easier walk would be to stay on the main road which went round the bottom of the hill. The road was lined with houses and lamps all the way. But to go that way would take much longer and it was already nearly one in the morning. Dad was cold, hungry and tired, and wanted to get home as fast as he could, even if it meant a hard, dark, lonely climb. And anyway, it was so foggy that the street-lamps weren't making much difference anyway. So Dad started climbing Turners Hill Lane.

Turners Hill Lane is so steep that Dad had only climbed a little way before he stepped right out of the fog into bright, freezing moonlight. The black road was covered in glittering frost patterns. Overhead the sky was clear and black, filled with brilliant stars and a big white moon.

He looked back down the lane, and there was the fog below him, all grey, blotting out the valley, blotting out all the street-lights and house-lights. It was as if the only things that existed in the world were that hillside and my dad, alone on it.

When he went on up the hill, his footsteps were sharp and clear, no longer muffled by the fog. Streamers and wisps of fog blew past him – there was a bit of a breeze up there on the hill and it was tearing the fog-bank into these long grey scarves.

Dad thought that now he was out of the fog, he'd get on faster, and he started stepping out. It was then that he heard Padfoot.

The roadway of the lane was narrow, just wide enough for a car, and it was black tarmac. The grass of the hedgerows grew right up to the tarmac on either side. Dad was walking on the road alongside one of these grass verges, and the dog was walking on the grass by the side of him: pad, pad, pad.

Dad looked round for the dog and didn't see it – but he wasn't too surprised. The moonlight was bright, but moonlight's tricky. You think it's bright and clear and you can see fine – but then you come to look closely at something and you find that everything's grey and misty, and you can't see as well as you thought you could. So Dad looked round for somebody who was out walking their dog – and there was nobody.

He could still hear the dog, pad, pad, pad by his side. Who would be walking the dog at that time in the morning, in that kind of weather? The dog was out by itself, just wandering around.

He looked for it again. He wasn't looking for a dog so much as for movement. The dog was walking with him, keeping up, and even if it was dark-coloured and blending into the hedgerow shadows, he'd see its movement. A leaf flickered in the wind. There was nothing bigger. No dog. But he could hear it.

Dad stopped. The dog stopped too. It was as if it had sat down, waiting for him. But he couldn't see it.

He walked on again, and the dog walked with him, pad, pad, pad.

What is it? Dad thought. He was looking all round him, trying to spot something that might be making a noise anything like that. There were only trees and breeze and darkness. Could his own footsteps somehow be echoing? Could the breeze rattling twigs somehow make a noise like that? He knew there was only one thing made that noise – something broad and soft and heavy treading down the frosty grass, pad, pad, pad.

He'd already thought of Padfoot. He knew the stories of the ghost dog, even if he didn't believe them. He knew that if you met Padfoot, it meant you were going to die soon.

Idiot! he thought. It's a sound being carried from somewhere else on the wind. It only *sounds* as if it's by the side of me.

He'd started walking faster without meaning to, and the dog kept up with him easily. It didn't seem to be hurrying, and it didn't sound even a little bit like anything but the paws of a big dog, pad, pad, pad. Dad knew, as well, that the sound wasn't being carried from anywhere else: it was right there at his side. And it was scaring him.

He thought: maybe all the people who talk about ghosts are right after all. He'd always thought that grown people who believed in ghosts were daft – fools who couldn't think straight. But here he was, walking with a ghost. Maybe this was the night he found out who the fool really was.

He kept looking down at the road, trying to *make* his eyes see the dog that *had* to be there. But there was no dog to be seen. Just the pad, pad, pad of its paws.

Dad wasn't just cold outside now. The cold was inside him too. Padfoot, the Death Dog, was going to follow him home, pad, pad, pad right to his door – and through it. He followed me home – can we keep him?

He reached the top of the hill, and started going down the other side. Pad, pad, pad went the paws on the grass. Ahead, Dad could see the other street-lamp, the one at the other end of Turners Hill Lane. Once past that lamp, he'd be on the Oakham Road, and another ten or fifteen minutes' walk, mostly downhill, would bring him home.

Dad started running, and his own footsteps were so loud on the hard cold road that he couldn't hear whether Padfoot was keeping up with him or not. He got to the lamp – and stopped and turned round. He looked back down the lane, to try and see the dog one last time.

This long, narrow black road stretched out behind him, glittering with frost in the moonlight, edged by tall black hedges. He couldn't see a thing moving. But as soon as he stopped he could hear the dog again: pad, pad, pad. And then, splat. A big, cold splash of water on his bald head, sending a shiver right down his back. He looked up – and got another big splash in the eye.

He was standing on the grass, which meant he was right under the telegraph wires. The freezing fog, being blown up from the valley, was condensing on the wires and falling off in big cold droplets, which fell into the frosty grass and went pad, pad, pad, pad.

Which was why the ghostly dog had kept up with my dad so effortlessly, without changing its pace – whether he walked fast or slow, he could always hear the water that was falling just beside him, pad, pad, pad. And that's why the dog stopped when Dad did – because the water had stopped dripping from that stretch of wire for the moment.

So there was my dad, on a freezing cold night, something after one in the morning, standing under a street-lamp in the deserted Turners Hill Lane, laughing his head off.

Then he got off down the hill, and home. His dinner was waiting for him, between two plates, keeping warm over a saucepan of simmering water.

My dad told this story often to my brother and sister and me, especially when we were worried about ghosts. He knew a thing or two about ghosts, he said: he'd gone walkies with Padfoot.

Black Dog

If you're in need of a well-earned break in peaceful English countryside, you could do a lot worse than look up 'Heritage Holidays'. They rent properties in all parts of the country, ranging from flats in mansions to converted weaver's lofts, old chapels and farm-labourer's cottages. All have been discreetly modernised to provide comfort and convenience without compromising the character of the building.

I plumped for a small cottage of grey stone on the outskirts of the tiny village of Kirkby Brade. Our cottage couldn't have been more perfect. It was surrounded by beautiful country walks, was in sight of the sea, and stood in its own pretty garden where we picked blackcurrants from the bushes.

Inside, the stone flags on the floor of the kitchen, and the rough plastered walls gave a homely feel. There was a well-appointed bathroom and kitchen, and central heating if you fancy a winter rent. The well-chosen furnishings achieved modern comfort while preserving the period mood.

The centre of social activity in Kirkby Brade is, of course, the pub, where visitors find a warm welcome. But the winding lanes, the long stretches of almost deserted beach, and the patches of ancient woodland provide plenty of entertainment for those seeking a get-away-from-it-all break. There is a beautiful little church, dating from the fifteenth century, and the village even has its own quaint old English custom. Close beside the churchyard's north wall is a faint bump in the grass, pointed out to me by the Vicar. This was, he said, 'the black dog's grave' and local children put flowers on it. Indeed, as we leaned on the wall in the sun, there were a couple of roses lying on the 'grave'.

*   *   *

On the 17th April, in the year of Our Lord, ——, a woman of the neighbourhood came to my door, begging that I should come at once. It was yet early and I had barely broken my fast, but I put on my coat and went with her, for by what she told me I judged the case to be urgent.

She brought me to the cottage where lived J——— B——, a small-holder. The cottage was an ugly thing of two storeys, built of grey stone, in view of the sea, which made its endless, comfortless moan at a distance. I knew B——, and his life of ceaseless work for little reward; and knew too the great grief that had come upon him. A bare month had passed since his wife had died in giving birth, and a mere two days since the babe had followed its dam into Eternity.

The neighbour-woman who was my guide made no approach to the door but led me hurriedly round the side of the house to the little yard behind. There, on the hard ground, in the drizzle and the cold wind from the sea, lay the bereaved husband and father.

Let those who talk of the fine sensitivities of the well-bred, and the boorishness of the commoner consider this scene. Here was a man who spent his life in labour, who could with difficulty write his name, but could scarcely read, and who must have been judged hardly better than a beast by any cultured company. Though I had baptised him at the font, and known him all his life, I think I never heard him speak more than a dozen words, and those mostly, 'Aye,' or 'Nay.' He was one who would stand among his fellows, smiling now and then, and nodding, but keeping his silence. A figure strong and well-made, a face pleasant enough, mostly by virtue of its youth, but nothing either of appearance or mind to raise him above the commonest.

And yet this young man, this common earthenware of humanity, lay on the hard ground in the cold rain, because his wife and babe were dead: when I have known others of a supposedly finer-grain throw off such matters in a day or two, with a few tears and sighs. The neighbour-woman said to me, 'I'm feared his mind's gone, sir.'

'No such thing,' said I, with a frown, for I would not have her setting such a tale free. 'Is it to be wondered at if the poor lad is distraught?' I asked her. 'He has seen everything he works for taken – but we will pray for him and God will send him strength to endure.'

I went and stood above the man and spoke his name. There was no manner of response. He lay sprawled almost on his belly, one arm folded beneath him and the other hand resting, in a fist, near his face. With no pillow to his head, his neck was cricked somewhat as it bent to let his head rest on the ground; the whole position being one of some discomfort. His eyes appeared to be open and staring, though unseeingly. At long intervals I caught a slow flicker of the lids and lashes.

'How long has he been thus?' I asked the woman, for I could not imagine any lying in such a comfortless place for many minutes together.

'I found him like that when I come by at first peep,' she said, which meant above an hour at least. 'He hasn't moved a limb,' she said.

Elderly and stiff though I was, I got down upon my knees, and placed my hand on his shoulder. 'J———, my boy.'

He breathed, and there was a slow blink of the one eye I could see, but that was all his answer. It was as though he was alone, as if he had not been touched, as if no one had spoken.

It was my most earnest desire to bring comfort to this poor soul, and accordingly, I sat upon the hard, wet ground. A cold chill struck up into my bones. How much colder, then, must he be, who had lain there an hour? His hair was wet from the drizzle; his coat, when I laid my hand on his shoulder, soaked.

I began to speak of his grief, telling him that I knew of it, and understood and even shared it. A due sorrow, I said, he must feel:

but despair he must avoid. God's ways seemed harsh to us often, and sometimes it was hard for us to understand that God was Love, but he must believe that his loved ones were now with Love. Nothing could ever hurt them again, and he must take comfort from that.

I spoke a prayer, and asked him to join me. I asked him to get up now, and to come with me into the house. All the time I squeezed his shoulder with my hand, or patted it; and all the time the rain drizzled upon me and made my clothes heavy with water which also trickled down my face and neck. My nose and my ears grew sore with cold, and my finger-ends were nipped. My old joints grew stiff, and I thought again how, if I suffered so in the little space I had sat there, in how much worse a case he must be. And yet he seemed indifferent to all: to the weather and to me.

'My poor boy,' I said, 'you must get up now. Come! Up with you! Spare a thought for my old carcase and don't make me stay out here in the rain any longer. Let me bring you into the house and a fire.'

Through all that time, through all my talking and all my friendly little touches on his shoulder, despite the cold and the rain, I will swear he never moved, except for his breathing – which was very shallow – and the occasional lifting or lowering of the one eye-lid I could see. Only one sound did he make, and that was when his breath was suddenly snatched in a long, fluttering whistle – as if his lungs had snatched at air of their own volition.

The morning was wearing on, and the rain was still falling, and my own discomfort was growing severe. So I began to upbraid him, thinking that harsh words might move him more than sympathy. Was this manly? I asked. Was this the way to do his wife's memory honour? Had he no self-respect?

'Yours is a common grief,' said I, 'that everyone feels. Must you make this great show? I tell you, it smacks of the Scribe and the Pharisee, of the Whited Sepulchre.'

He lay as he had lain all along, his eyes now closed, and with no visible stirring of breath. The woman, wrapping her shawl around her, bent over him and added her pleas to mine, saying, 'Get up now, my love; come on, don't lie in the wet no more. Here's me and Vicar getting wet for no good reason, and it's doing no good for anybody,' said she, very sensibly. 'Come on, come in now and have something to eat.'

I asked her if she knew when J——— had last eaten.

'He et nothing all day yesterday, that I know for sure,' she said.

'Well, it's clear that talking is of no use,' said I. 'And all this while he's been getting wetter and colder. Help me with him, won't you?'

She came willingly to my aid and, between us, we essayed to lift our young friend up from the ground.

I had hoped that, once lifted up, he might come to himself and go with us, but I had mistaken. He did not resist us, but gave us no help, and was as heavy and limp as a sack of grain. If we hauled up his shoulders from the wet ground, then his head and arms hung down and dragged him back towards it. We could not get his legs beneath him, and he would not stand. As soon as we relaxed our efforts, then he sank back to the earth again. It was no work for an elderly man and a woman, and soon she and I were gasping for breath and muddied almost from head to foot. Any onlooker must have been moved to laughter: but the good woman and I were far from such.

For myself, much though I pitied the lad's bereavement, I was growing furious with his stubbornness, and this unseemly display of a grief much better kept private. I did not believe it possible that our exhortations and efforts were unheard and unseen. We had hauled him half-upright once more, and he was propped against the good woman, who breathed hard. So angry was I that I made so bold as to take his face in my hand, to make him listen if I could.

'J———,' said I, 'I think you would be ashamed to put us to so much trouble. Enough of this, my boy. I want you to get up on your feet and come inside with me.'

Yet my voice faded as I spoke, for I was looking in his face, which was that of a sleep-walker. His eyes were open, and blinked slowly at long intervals, but stared away from me. Not a lineament of his face gave the least sign, not the least quiver, of being aware of anything that passed around him. He hung in our grip like a scarecrow.

An inner cold ran through me then, more chill than the wind that blew upon me. For the first time I gave some belief to what the woman had said: that his senses were gone, that this was no man, but an empty shell.

I turned his face directly to mine, so that he must look into my eyes. He did not resist me, but at once his eyes shifted slightly, so that he looked beyond me. I turned his face again, and again his gaze shifted.

Aha, thought I, there is a mind here: and I pulled his head back and bent over him so that he must look at me, try as he might. And then he looked at me, and looked through me, as if I were a pane of glass, until his eyes closed and shut out even my transparency.

'Lay him down,' I said to my companion, and we did, though she, good woman, pillowed his head in her lap. 'He must be got indoors,' I said, 'and it's plain that the task is beyond we two. Can you find some others, do you think, who could help us carry him inside?'

She said she could and, staying only to fold her shawl into a bundle and place it beneath his head, she rose and hurried away.

I went into the house, finding it a damp cave, as cold as the yard, for the door was standing open. No fire had been lit in the hearth for a while: the ashes were quite cold.

There was a little kindling and wood in a basket, and I promised myself that I should build a fire – but first I went through the kitchen and into the small parlour. I paused there a moment, glancing about at its bare neatness: the poor furniture polished so well and covered with cloths, the few ugly little ornaments of glazed chalk. The woman who had kept it so would never be seen or heard again on this earth, and I felt something of the pang it must give him every time he opened this door.

I passed through the sad little room and climbed the steep stairs in the corner, to the two small rooms above. They held little more than a bed and a chair. From the bed I took the coverlet and carried it down again, and out into the yard.

J——— had rolled away from the shawl we had placed under his head and lay as he had at first, with his eyes closed. I wasted no breath on him, but dropped the coverlet over him, and replaced the shawl beneath his head. Then I went back inside and busied myself with lighting a fire, for once we had J——— in the house, we should need to warm him.

Once the fire was crackling and beginning to burn up, I went out into the yard again, to discover that J——— had cast the coverlet from him, and had moved enough to leave the shawl-pillow behind, so that he once more lay with cricked neck, leaning his temple on the hard ground.

'Well, my friend,' said I, as I stood above him, 'you are not quite as unaware as you would have us think.' Accordingly, I lifted his head and put the shawl back beneath it, and once more threw the coverlet over him; and I stood on watch. For a time during which I suppose I might have counted slowly to twenty, he made no movement. Then he flung up his arm and tossed the coverlet from him, and rolled over so that he lay as before, but upon his other side, and without the shawl beneath his head. But having done that, he sank again into immobility, and gave no flicker of response when I spoke his name, nor when I stooped and touched him.

Well, thought I to myself, if you can choose to throw off a coverlet, you can choose to come back to us. My hopes rose. A little warmth, thought I, and the scent of food; some warmed milk and brandy, and we should soon win him over.

Soon after that our good neighbour returned, bringing with her four other good neighbours, all strong men; and as soon as they understood the sad case of our young friend they wasted no time on speculation, but lifted him up bodily between them and – he making no resistance whatsoever – carried him into the kitchen of his home in a moment.

Well, we laid him down before the hearth on a bit of rag-rug that lay there, and, stripping off his wet coat, bundled the damp coverlet about him in such a way that it shielded him from the draughts, but not from the heat of the fire. One man set the kettle on the hob to boil, and my friend, the good wife, ran up the stairs to come back with a pillow from the bed, which she placed under J————'s head. I asked another neighbour to step up the road with a message to my wife, if he would be so good, asking for some delicacies which might tempt the appetite of one disinclined to eat.

I was moved by the kindness, even tenderness, shown by these labouring men, who might have been thought hardened by work and poverty, and who had no education to widen their understanding or soften their sympathies. And yet, gathering about the hearth, they set themselves to make gentle, coaxing conversation, such as might yet draw a response from him slumped apathetically on the flags. The eldest of these men – who was, indeed, old enough to have fathered the lad – seated himself on the floor, gently stroked

J————'s forehead with his thick finger-ends, and addressed him thus:'Shall we get thee a bit to eat, eh? Say, "aye" – come on, don't carry on like this. Her wouldn't want thee to, would her? How about a drop of ale? How about we mull it? Say, "aye". Tell Davey, "aye", come on. Tell me to sling me hook then, but let's have a word out o'thee, even if it's "shut your gob".'

I seated myself on a rickety old kitchen chair and observed closely. At first J————'s eye was open and fixed on some spot a few inches in front of him – on some ember from the fire, or some crack in the hearth-flags. Then his eye closed, and no word that was spoken, no kind touch won any notice or further movement from him.

The good wife cut bread into slices, and one of the men toasted it, and a platter of it, spread with dripping, was set on the hearth before J————'s face – and at that he suddenly raised his arms and rolled right over, turning his back to the hearth, the food and the men, and folding his arms over his head, so as to cover his eyes and to smother from sight his whole face. In this new posture he fell into his former stillness; nor did he make a sound.

At this juncture my own good wife appeared, bringing with her brandy and fresh milk, fresh bread and butter and other good things.

The men who had been gathered round the hearth had seemingly been much startled by J————'s sudden, silent turning from them. They now rose and came about us, their faces anxious and questioning. We all adjourned into the yard, though it drizzled still; leaving J———— in the kitchen.

There we took counsel. It was the notion of Davey, the eldest of the men, that we should simply leave J——— to himself until the fit wore itself out. 'I feel for the lad,' he said, 'but he'll eat when he gets hungry enough.' And to this we all agreed. Accordingly all went about their own business, though with many doubts, and only I remained, since it was my duty. I went back into the kitchen, and sat on a chair by the hearth, to keep the fire burning (one of the men had said he would bring in a further supply of fuel). J——— lay on the floor at my feet.

I had not been alone with him for half an hour when he abruptly and silently rose up, on his hands and knees, and *crawled* across the kitchen as if he had not the strength to rise to his feet. I can hardly say why, but to see him crawl like that made the hair prickle on the back of my neck. It raised in me a feeling absolutely of repulsion. The line of his back as he crawled, and his head upraised to see his way, put me in mind of an animal going upon four feet. It brought the fear of madness on me.

From my chair, I watched. On reaching the door, he leaned against it, raising himself wearily until he could reach the latch. He then dropped to the floor and waited until the door swung inwards. On hands and knees he negotiated it and disappeared, crawling, into the yard.

I rose from my chair and followed. He lay in the yard, in the cold mud and drizzle, but now in his shirt-sleeves and upon his back with his arms folded about his head.

Now I truly began to fear for the outcome. This stubbornness was not like the man. Never before had he been notable for any such displays, never one to play to the gallery or seek for the attention of his neighbours. Rather had he been quiet, even shy, one to draw back from attention, embarrassed by it.

This, thought I to myself, is no outward show. This is the shape of his mind showing itself plainly in his actions – as a man delighted might laugh and clap his hands, or a man angered bang his fist down on a table.

So what is the mind here displayed, I asked myself? This seeking for the hardest, coldest bed, away from shelter and warmth: this turning from his fellows, his steadfast refusal to see them or hear them or in any way acknowledge their presence – what does it figure?

It smacked of despair, certainly – but surely this was despair run to madness – and I was chilled inwardly.

I was, for a while, at a loss what to do. I could not bring him back indoors by myself, and I was reluctant to take my neighbours from their work again. Perhaps, thought I, he feels that he must do this and, just as he will eat when hunger becomes sharp enough, so he will come to the fire when the cold bites too deep. So I brought my chair to the doorway and sat there, looking out into the yard.

There I sat, suffering degrees of anxiety and pity as the day wore on. I can bear witness that during all that time, J———— did not move. I asked myself: was he aware of my presence, and was that awareness bolstering his will? If I had gone, and left him, would he have given up this strange behaviour and come in to his own fireside of his own will? But my conscience would not let me take the risk of putting it to the test.

When the afternoon light began to turn pewter, and the chill of the day turn frosty, I went to call my neighbours again, and we lifted him up and carried him in once more to the fire. We took counsel among ourselves and quickly agreed that he could not be left, for what if, during the night, he crawled into the yard? The night that was coming would be cold, and we doubted that morning would find him alive if he lay out in it.

As I was more elderly than my neighbours, and in a more sedentary employment, I needed the less sleep, and volunteered to sit through the night in the cottage. That good man Davey, to my pleasure, agreed to keep me company. 'Well, do you sleep,' said I, 'and I will wake you if it's needful.'

So, after our other neighbours had left, we built up the fire, Davey and me, and sat across the hearth from each other, with J———— lying on the floor between us, wrapped up in the coverlet from the bed. We ate and drank, and Davey made some attempt to coax J———— into eating, pulling his arms away from his face and holding bread to his mouth. He might have been holding it to the lips of a statue: the eyes remained closed and the whole face as still as if carven. But I was amazed when Davey dribbled ale on to J————'s mouth, and there was still no flicker of response. I had thought there must be some involuntary movement then, to swallow or to lick the lips, but there was nothing. He allowed the liquid to run over his face and neck.

'I am amazed,' I whispered, 'at the strength of will.'

'Always a powerful will, that one,' Davey said – which I was surprised to hear, but it may be that Davey knew him better than I. 'I don't like to think of it now,' says Davey.

I will be short with my story, and tell you that J———— made no escape into the yard that night, and I dozed in my chair, waking from the cold when the fire began to burn down, and Davey went upstairs and slept on the bed after I had made fresh promises that I would call him if necessary.

But morning brought little hope, for there was J———— lying in the middle of the room, uncovered, his back to the fire, and it quite impossible to tell whether he was asleep or merely withdrawn from us as he had been for so many hours. I felt his face and hands and, though chilled, he was not dangerously cold. Still, it was now two whole days since he had eaten or drunk the smallest bit or drop, and he was white as plaster, even to his lips, though the shadows beneath his eyes were as though someone had daubed ink there with their thumbs.

When our other neighbours came in and found him in this poor state, a sort of desperation came to them. They hauled him upright, though he sagged in their hold, and pushed spoonfuls of porridge into his face. It was as if they tried to feed one asleep, or a rag doll. If ever they managed to get some portion of what was on the spoon into his mouth, then it slithered out again, because he would not swallow.

Then so fierce did my friends become in their determination

that, having pushed porridge into J————'s mouth, one gripped his chin to hold his mouth closed and another pinched his nose. I was dismayed by this violence, but held my tongue 'til I saw what good might come of it.

To be sure J———— struggled a little. He raised one hand, he tried to turn his head, he kicked: but then he seemed to relax in their hold, and I thought they had killed him. 'Stop, stop!' I cried. 'Stop, I beg you!'

They released him, and his mouth opened, and the porridge slithered down his chin. We all of us looked at each other in astonishment. Never had any of us known such strength of will, such stubbornness, bent on self-destruction. I had not thought it possible.

The man holding the porridge bowl and spoon – I shall not name him – set them aside and slapped J———— hard across the face. J————'s eyes opened, as if in shock at the blow; but before we could hope, they rolled shut again, and though he was struck twice more, until his white face reddened, he made no sound and no further sign that he even felt the smacks.

'What good does this do?' I cried, seizing the man's hand as he raised it yet again. 'Leave him be.'

The man who had struck the blows looked shame-faced. Those who held J———— up laid him down. He immediately covered his face with his arms and lay motionless. We all withdrew to the door and stood looking back at him.

'This,' said Davey, 'is the black dog, and no mistake.'

Mention of a dog brought vividly to my mind the image of J———crawling across the kitchen floor, and I almost shuddered. 'Come,' said I, 'let us have no such superstitious talk—' For the black dog they spoke of is a ghostly one which is supposed to dog a man's footsteps and bring him to despair. 'There are no ghosts here, but only a natural grief.'

They looked at me under their brows, as if to ask, was what they were witnessing *natural*?

* * *

Pain built into a sheltering wall.

Hunger-pain: griping belly and aching head: – build it into the wall.

Thirst: dry mouth and sore, narrow throat: – another stone in the wall.

Stinging of blows: – raise the wall.

Through the wall, nothing's seen.

Noise clacking, distant, on the wall's other side.

Draw away, lean to the cold . . .

Teach the eye to unsee. Let all merge and blur until no more is understood than when the eye stares through its own lid.

Teach the ear to unhear. Unmeaning of wind, of bird-song and sea-moan, jar of words. Unheeded, unravelling into brute, senseless noise.

Teach the flesh not to feel. Cold chills the flesh until it burns,
until cold and warmth and pain are the same, and nothing.
Sight, hearing, touch: let them go.
Easiest of all to give up, the tongue. Let it lie, a lump in the jaw.
Let its bulk seal the mouth. There's no use for it. There's nothing
to say.

After a weekend of peace, quiet, long walks, fresh air, and evenings in the pub, I took one last turn round the churchyard, left a fresh rose from the cottage garden on the black dog's grave, and drove back to town much refreshed. I heartily recommend all Heritage Holidays, but especially Kirkby Brade, to anyone who needs a break from today's frenetic rat-race.

* * *

Still now, many years later, I ask myself what we could have done, for if a man's will be that strong, you cannot force him to eat and drink: you can only choke him.

We kept the fire in, and we kept him by it. We wrapped him in the coverlet when he threw it off; we spoke to him; we begged him to eat. We got from him not one word nor one look.

What can we call such strength of will turned to such bad end? I cannot say whether he was mad, or whether he was possessed of a cold, bitter sanity that looked and saw there was nothing more for him in this world, and so turned from it. Day by day his strength failed, and though we drew him close to the fire and wrapped hot bricks in the coverlet with him, his hands and feet were still cold. We could not warm him, because he would not eat.

I took his face in my hands and shed tears on him as I begged him to eat. 'Don't make me have to bury you too,' I said. 'Are you satisfied, to have made an old man cry? Will you not listen to reason? This is sin, this is self-murder – In God's name and for God's sake, will you not save your own life and your own soul?'

It was as if I spoke to one in a deep sleep. Indeed, when I spoke those words, he may already have slipped into the deep sleep that often precedes death. I think that, towards the end, he could not have turned back from his road even had he wished. The deathly cold moved towards his heart; his breathing grew rough and faltering; and I woke from a doze in the cold of an early morning to find that the spirit had gone and left behind only a lump of flesh and bone that must be buried before it decayed.

I prayed passionately that morning; prayed that he might find whatever reunion he had desired, though this had been wilful self-slaughter.

Indeed, I found myself passionate. This had been a young man I had hardly known, though I had liked him well enough, and knew nothing to his discredit. But having passed through these days and nights with him, now that he was dead, I found that I had loved him, and felt such anger and such sorrow that I was shaken where I stood.

He may have found peace – I pray that, in God's Mercy, he

found peace – but he left none behind him. Davey wept and roared and beat his fists on the cottage walls. We who had sat with him and tried to save him were furious, and could not look at each other. We would turn our faces aside and go by without a word if we met in the street; and among those who had not come to help was a sort of silent shame. If any made to gossip about the death, their neighbours turned on them furious, silencing faces. Indeed, the stillness of his madness lay on our tongues for many weeks after his death and forever after, as far as talking of his death was concerned. His house stood empty and people stared hard at it as they went by. 'Black dog,' they said.

The funeral, if funeral it could be called, was attended only by Davey, my wife, and the good woman who had first fetched me. Look at it how you will, it was self-murder, and I could not permit him to be buried in the church-yard with his wife and babe. A grave was made for him outside the yard's wall, on the north side. I could not give him the burial service, but we few mourners stood beside the grave, and I spoke a prayer.

That night, I saw flowers had been left on the grave. Even now, so long after, children bring bunches of wild flowers and lay them on the unmarked mound.

And only last night I dreamed that I saw him crawling towards me on his hands and knees, though his eyes stared through me, as if he would crawl through me – and I woke in a cold horror that I could not explain and cannot forget.

The Baby

Emily loved the baby. Lying on her sofa, she'd hold her for hours. She'd talk to the baby and watch her sleep, sniff her skin, kiss her, rub her own cheek against the baby's soft one. She'd let the baby take her fingers in an almost unbreakable grip, and when the baby's bottle was prepared, Emily always begged to be allowed to feed her. She learned to put the baby on her shoulder and wind her. She'd hold the baby up in front of her and make its little woolly-booted feet dance on her belly, and coo at it, and rub foreheads with it. Maybe she loved it because it was even more helpless than she was herself.

Emily was my great-aunt, one of my grandfather's younger sisters. I never met her. She died long before I was born. But I've often been told the story of her and the baby.

She was born crippled. I don't know what was wrong with her: that wasn't in the story. What I was told was that Emily spent her whole life lying on a sofa in the hot, crowded, ugly little kitchen of her home.

I know just what the house would have been like: so many of my relatives lived in houses like it. Two rooms on the ground floor – a front room opening directly on to the street, and a back-kitchen opening directly on to the yard. The outside lavatory, the only lavatory – and they were lucky not to have to share it with any other families – was next to the kitchen door.

But it's the kitchen I want to tell you about. One wall was taken up with an old iron cooking-range. The fire in the grate was alight for cooking, regardless of the weather, summer and winter. On the hob would have stood a kettle that never got cold, and a teapot constantly brewing black tea. High over the range was a shelf – higher than head-height – and on this shelf would have been some cheap, ugly ornaments: black and white chalk dogs, won at fairs, and fluted glass vases in harsh tints of blue or pink. There was also a large clock, ticking heavily. Emily had probably stopped seeing them – except in moments of intense exasperation, when she noticed them again and hated them for still being there, and still being just the same.

The window would have been small, made up of square panes, and almost completely obscured by net curtain or – on washing day – by sheets of newspaper.

Into the rest of the room was crammed: a square kitchen table with drawers, and several straight-backed kitchen chairs; Emily's sofa; a big stone sink, almost deep enough to take a bath in; and an old armchair that Great-Granddad always sat in. There was so little room that most of this furniture touched other pieces at some point. Pulling out a chair to sit at the table was a difficult manoeuvre, especially if there were people sitting on the others.

The woodwork – including a skirting board that came halfway up the wall – would have been painted a dark brown, and the wallpaper would have been yellowed with age and tobacco-smoke, and spotted with large brown damp spots. All the men in the family smoked heavily: even Great-Gran smoked the nub ends on the quiet. So the room was always hung with a fog of greyish-yellow smoke, and the glass covers over the gas-lamps were coated with the smoke too, so the light was always dulled. The gas-lamps would hiss and sizzle, and smell of burning oil, and the clock went tock tock tock tock tock.

Somewhere, hanging on the wall, with its corners curling, was an old, out-of-date calendar, with a thick border of tartan pattern, and a picture inside the border of Highland cattle. There was always one of these calendars on the walls of those old rooms – or, if not a calendar, then an old biscuit tin with a picture of Highland cattle on the lid.

On the back of the kitchen door, which would have been of planking, painted brown, would have been hanging coats and scarfs, a great many of them, bulging into the room and taking up still more space.

This was the room in which Emily spent her life. She didn't

have a wheelchair: too expensive. This was before the National Health Service. I never heard of her going to school, or having lessons of any kind, or ever being taken out anywhere. She just lay on her sofa.

The sofa was an old one, sagging in the middle and knobbly with springs. Emily had several cushions, one a particularly hard one of pink satin, embroidered with a picture of a lady in a crinoline standing among hollyhocks. There was a cigarette burn in it. There was an old, black-striped pillow, in a white pillowcase with a blue stripe. She had a sheet under and over her, and various old blankets, washed and worn to thin felt. As a coverlet she always had an old tartan travel rug, covered with dog hairs and cat hairs. All the pillows, cushions, blankets, smelt of tobacco. In the winter they became dampened by condensation from the boiling kettle.

I don't think Emily would have been bothered by loneliness much. She came from a large family, who came and went freely, even after they'd left home. And Emily's mother, my Great-Gran, would have been with her most of the time, bad-temperedly clambering about the furniture, pouring another cup of tea every few minutes – 'You want one, Em?' – or putting the kettle on the fire again to make another pot. Or peeling potatoes in a bowl at the table, or scraping carrots, shelling peas, slicing green beans – no convenience foods in those days. Making them both cry by chopping onions. I suppose Emily would have been given a bowl of peas to shell, when they were in season.

Every Sunday the whole family would have turned up and crammed into the kitchen. Emily's father, brothers and uncles would have jammed themselves around the table, to drink beer and play cards. Sisters and sisters-in-law, aunts by blood and marriage, would have perched on Emily's sofa, in and on the armchair, on the draining board – or even have struggled past the chairs into the front room. Winter or summer, the sweat rolled down their faces, because the range-fire was burning. In the summer, the yard door stood open, and the family children ran up and down the yard and side-entry, screaming – and making Emily jealous.

Great-Gran moved between the range and the sink, fighting to take every step, because of the crowd. She would be swearing and threatening people, and snatching smokes from other people's cigarettes. The radio blared out; bets were shouted above its noise. If anyone wanted to leave the table, or go outside, then almost everyone else in the room had to move too, and they all complained loudly.

Emily was stuck in the middle of it. Maybe she enjoyed being in the middle of a gossiping crowd – but if she ever got tired of the noisy radio, or just bored with it playing tunes she didn't like – if she was oppressed by the crowd and the chatter

and the heat – if she ever just felt out of sorts – well, hard luck.
She couldn't get away.

I think she probably longed to be lonely. She must have
treasured those few times when even her mother was out, and
she could lie there on her sofa, leafing through a film magazine
someone had given her, although she could hardly read and
had never seen a film. She'd never been to the cinema, and
she'd probably never even heard of television. She'd certainly
never seen one. The clock would have gone tock tock tock
tock. And then the kitchen door would have been shoved
open, and one of her sisters or sisters-in-law would have come
in, shouting, 'Hello!'

Emily probably told them to clear off. She wasn't the sweet,
forbearing cripple you find in books. My aunt Mary, who
knew her, and has often told me about her, says she was
spiteful. Mary was a little girl at the time, younger than Emily,
and often saw her, because Mary used to go round to her
gran's every chance she got. But she kept as far away from
Emily as she could because, she says, Emily would pull the
hair of visiting children, and pinch them on the sly, and
then, when they cried, say, loudly, 'What's the matter with
you?' Of course, if any of them pinched her back, or hit her,
they got into terrible trouble, 'because the poor girl's a
cripple.' The dog and cat kept away from her too, because
she teased them all the time. She'd pinch the dog until it

yelped, and then say, 'What's the matter with it? Fleas again!'

She would answer her mother and other adults back in a way that Mary, at the time, thought really shocking. 'Oh, why don't you put a sock in it?' she'd say, or, to a visitor, 'That's the sixth cup of tea and the third slice of cake you've had. You won't have room for your tea when you go home.'

Great-Gran had a notoriously filthy temper – she used to hit people with the flat of her sharp carving knife – but she never said a word about Emily's rudeness. Yet if Mary, or anyone else, said the slightest little thing out of turn – such as daring to ask if there was any more milk – Great-Gran would turn on them, waving the carving-knife and saying, 'I'll have the fats of your eyes on the point of this!'

Mary – and the other grandchildren – disliked Emily. They thought she was spoiled. Mary was always glad to see the cat scratch her. It was the only member of the household that ever got its own back on Emily.

But I was telling you about the baby.

It was Emily's niece, the daughter of one of her elder sisters. I may not have all the facts quite right, but I think the husband was away, trying to find work and, as his wife was heavily pregnant, she moved home to be with her mother. It must have been quite a crush in that little house, but those were the days when people expected to sleep several to a bed, and even on mattresses on the floor.

The elder sister gave birth to her baby in the house – that must have been a major upheaval too. Emily would have lain downstairs on her sofa while all the fuss went on upstairs. Something else for her to envy, perhaps. How would she ever get married or have children? But the baby was carried downstairs for her to see – having first been carried up a few steps of a ladder in the bedroom, to ensure that it would rise in the world. Emily loved the baby.

About three weeks after the baby's birth, its mother was found dead in bed. She'd had a brain embolism. She'd been fine when she'd gone to bed the night before. But in the night her brain had gone pop! and there she was, the new mother, dead. Not the first child my great-gran had lost, nor the last.

So the care of the baby fell to Great-Gran – and to Emily. For the first months of its life, she had it to lie on the sofa with her, and watched it sleep, and fed it. As it grew older, she played peek-a-boo with it over the edge of the tartan coverlet. She talked to it, and tickled it, and tried to teach it to say her name. She wanted her name to be the first word it said.

She was jealous of other people holding the baby, and always wanted her back after a couple of minutes. The baby filled her life, until it died. I don't know why the baby died. The story hasn't passed that down. Since there would have been no way of sterilising the feeding-bottle except by boiling, perhaps gastroenteritis was the cause. I only know that it died. All the story says about the effect of its death on Emily is that 'she missed it.'

While everyone else went to the funeral, she would have lain on the sofa in the brown, tobacco-fogged, dim kitchen that smelled of old frying and stubbed cigarettes. She listened to the clock going tock tock tock tock tock, and she missed the baby. At night, when the rest of the family were upstairs, she lay under her blankets in the dark kitchen and listened to the clock tick. Two brothers had died in that house, one as a baby, one in childhood. And the elder sister, the baby's mother. And now the baby. The corners of the room must have seemed inhabited.

For two more years Emily lay on her sofa in the kitchen, and missed the baby. Then she died herself. She was thirteen.

All these deaths may seem far-fetched to you, even a little comical. But if you were poor in the thirties, you didn't have as many defences against death as people have now. Several deaths in a family weren't so uncommon. I don't know for sure why Emily died, any more than I know why she was crippled: the story doesn't say. One aunt says that she thinks she 'always had a weak heart and it just gave out'. That's probably so.

The family knew Emily was dying, and carried her upstairs and put her in a proper bed. They carried straight-backed chairs up from the kitchen and set them by the bed, so they could keep her company in the little bedroom.

It was winter, and dark. The window was a square of black night. There was a kerosene lamp lit, and hissing, and its light reflected in the blackness of the window against the night outside. Great-Gran was closest to the bed, holding Emily's hand. A couple of her other daughters, and a daughter-in-law sat on the other chairs.

They sat listening to Emily's breathing getting harder, and harsher. Her hand was getting cold in her mother's. And then Emily said, 'Open the window!'

'You don't want the window open,' the daughter-in-law said. 'It's cold.'

'Open the window! I want – the window open!'

So the daughter-in-law went to the window and pretended to open it, but didn't. 'There you are. The window's open now.'

Emily was quiet for a short while. Then she said, 'You didn't open the window – open it! Open it!'

They looked at each other, but no one went to the window. It would be bad for Emily, they thought, to let the cold in; and she didn't know what she was talking about.

But then Emily began to struggle to raise herself in the bed. 'Open –! Let her in! She wants to come in!'

They looked at each other again. But dying people wander in their minds. They didn't expect her to make sense. Great-

Gran was trying to calm Emily and get her to lie down.

'She's outside,' Emily said. 'The baby! Let her in. Open the window – let her in.'

Everyone looked at the window. Its wooden bars framed panes of blackness, brilliantly reflecting the lamp. Nothing else. What else could be out there, outside the window of an upper room?

'She's knocking at the window! Let her in!'

The others in that room – Great-Gran, her daughters, the daughter-in-law – felt their hearts squeezed and stared at each other with frozen faces. The daughter-in-law, sitting near the window with her back to it, rose and scuttled to crouch by her sisters-in-law, but didn't dare to look at the window, for fear of seeing the baby hanging there, white against the black sky, and rapping at the glass with its little fist.

Emily was still trying to raise herself. She was growing frantic and choking. 'Let her in! Let her in!'

Great-Gran left the bed, went to the window and, after struggling with the stiff frame, raised it. In came a stream of chill, damp air – but nothing else that anyone but Emily could see.

Emily saw something. They saw her looking at whatever it was, above her. She died a moment after that. Great-Gran left the window open until late the next day. She wanted to be sure that Emily, and the baby, had gone.

This is just a story to you. To me, it's family. It's true. I never hear it without feeling that cold pressure on the scalp, that touch on the back, that grue of dread. I wonder, when the time comes, when I have to lie in my body and feel it die around me, will that baby come to me, with its little blue face and clutching little hands? Will it come riding in Emily's arms?

130

There was a silence. For a moment everyone had forgotten themselves. Then the director remembered to yell, 'Okay – cut!'

Chatter broke out, laughter. People moved, breathed deeper, scratched their heads, ears, noses, but kept their places, ready to go again. The director called out to the camera and sound crews and, when they reported that everything was fine, raised both hands above his head and shouted, 'It's a wrap!'

People whistled and cheered. Someone started to clap, a small pattering sound almost lost in the big sound-stage. Others joined in and the sound grew louder, spreading. There was stamping, rebel-yells. Sound technicians, lighting crews, cameramen, make-up, the hardest audience of all to please, all applauding. It wasn't merely surprise and self-congratulation at having wrapped an important scene on only the second take. They were applauding Will.

It had been quite a performance. Even Debs, who liked to look at her clients through unstarred eyes, had felt her hair move. The crew probably appreciated more that Will hadn't kept them waiting, had been word-perfect, and had hit every mark. They might be quitting on time tonight, and they might never witness anything like it again. Not even from him.

Debs stood straighter, smiling, and looked round at the enthused faces, the beating hands. She felt like bowing graciously, accepting her share of the applause. She deserved it. Without her eye for talent, and her persistence and hard work, Will wouldn't be in front of the camera.

Will, not looking at anyone, fiddled with the ring in his ear as he went over to the director, affecting to believe that the applause was nothing to do with him. The director, a saggy teddy-bear of a man whose mop of grey hair hardly reached Will's shoulder, took his arm and turned him towards the clapping, so he had no choice but to acknowledge it.

Debs, watching Will and knowing him, thought that he didn't know whether to admit to being pleased, or to run away. He turned, as the director insisted, and looked shiftily at the applauding crew, turned red, for a moment looked as if he was going to cry, then grinned and tried nodding as if he was used to this every day – but with one hand raised to partially hide his face. Finally, after a word more with the director, he did run away, hurrying from the set, his head down, his hand pushing through his hair.

Debs moved to meet him, but he was caught by a crewman who wanted his autograph. As she waited, handbag under her arm, Debs heard a young woman say to her friend, 'He's incredible.'

'He can act a bit too.' The two young women laughed.

Others had joined the original autograph-hunter, and Debs had to wait. Whenever it seemed that there was only one more person waiting for Will to sign their scrap of paper, another would come up. Some, Debs guessed, were hardened old technicians who had nearly as good an eye for talent as she did, and were investing in an autograph they might be able to sell at a nice profit in a few years' time. Others just wanted an excuse to get close to Will and talk to him. And he wasn't helping matters by being so approachable, so animated and charming. He was calling people to him like a beacon.

Hanging her bag on her shoulder, Debs plunged into the gathering circle of autograph hunters and gripped Will by the arm. As he gave her a big smile and stooped towards her, she caught his chin in her hand and kissed his cheek – just to show the onlookers who had prior claim here. 'I'm sorry, darlings, but I have to take Will away now. I'm sorry, I'm sorry,' she repeated, as those who hadn't yet collected autographs pressed closer. Retreating, she towed Will with her. 'Appointments, I'm afraid.'

When they were clear, she said, 'Don't you remember, darling? Meet the press time.'

He spun half away from her hold on his arm, exaggeratedly,

clutching at his head. 'God! No!' His eyes were bright, his face flushed – he was high on performing and praise and applause. Skittish. Not, perhaps, the best circumstances under which to bring him and the alligators together.

'We'll take a few minutes out first,' she said, patting his arm. 'Have a drink.' Not coffee. No stimulants, thank you. A couple of beers would quieten him down nicely. And he would never know he was being quietened down, that was the charm of it.

'I'm very pleased to meet you, Will.'

'Pleased to meet you.'

'It's very good of you to see me.'

'Good of you to come and talk to me.'

'If we could start –?'

'Sure.'

'Haven't much time. Could I ask you – looking forward in time, for the moment, if I may – how do you feel about playing Dean?'

'I'm just glad I got the part. It's a great opportunity for me, a very good script.'

'I heard that you went along to Dean's home-town –? And that there were all these reports of Dean's ghost being seen – by people who'd known him – but that it turned out to have been you.'

114

Will slid down in his chair. His right ankle came up to rest on his left knee, and he folded his arms. 'Never happened.'

'But I was told by—'

'Never happened.'

'But you do look astonishingly like him.'

'I don't think so.'

'Oh, you do.'

'I don't look like him at all.'

'But you *do*. I mean, surely it was a factor in your getting the part?'

Will dipped still lower in his chair, his arms still more tightly folded. Twisting, he looked at Debs. 'Didn't being able to act have something to do with it?'

'Well! Right. This is nice. First question then, Will. What's it like being the most beautiful man in the world?'

There was a long sigh from Will. He lowered his boot from the knee it rested on to the floor and hitched up straighter in his chair. Debs contained a sigh of her own. Perhaps four beers would have been better?

'You'd have to ask him,' Will said.

'Oh, come on – you have to be aware you've been called that.'

Will fidgeted. 'Called what?'

'Well, "the most beautiful man in the world", of course.'

'I've been called a lot of stupid things.' Fidgeting again, he cast a look at the journalist which seemed to suggest that stupid things called him stupid things.

'Yeah, right. How about "prickly"?'

Debs leaned over from her chair and said, 'Perhaps you could ask Will something about the film?'

'Darling,' Debs said, 'have another beer, and try not to pick a quarrel with the next one, hmm? Let it go! They're only parasites. We just have to put up with them.'

'Will! Pleased to meet you. Let me just tell you – the first thing I saw you in was that low-budget piece, "Ontario".'

'Yeah?'

'Superb! Very under-rated. I for one want to thank you for it. Your performance was just amazing.'

'Thank you.'

'Was it your first starring –?'

'It was, yeah, it was.'

'Hard to believe. Remarkably assured. And nuanced. You brought out so many sides of the character. I mean, he was so focused and so hard-bitten, but you could always see how vulnerable he was.'

'Well, I tried—'

'I remember making a note of your name. I thought you

were an actor to watch – but now of course you're the most beautiful man in the world.'

Will nodded. Got up. Walked across the room, opened the door into the next, went through it and slammed it after him.

'I'm sorry!' Will said. 'I'm sorry, I'm sorry! Okay? I'm sorry. But I hate it. Hate it hate it hate it hate it. Will, Will, Will – they all call me "Will", like they all know me, and I don't know *any* of them. It makes me feel like–' He came to rest against a wall with his hands braced on either side of a mirror, and stared into the eyes of his reflection.

Debs put down the phone. She had ordered sandwiches and a bottle of wine – beer having failed – to give them a break. There had to be a break, even if it meant interviews running late or being cancelled. Every encounter was winding Will up tighter. It was something that always amazed her: the way some personalities could expand on stage or in front of a camera, become ten feet tall and blindingly charismatic – and then, off-stage, away from the camera, shrink, become fidgety, tongue-tied. Shy. Awkward.

'Like I'm stark-bollock-naked in the middle of a stage and I've forgotten my lines.'

'What, darling?'

'That's how they make me feel.' He was staring into the

mirror. 'And it's not *true*. I don't look like Dean. I'm *not* beautiful.'

Coming up behind him, she put her hand on his warm back, and they looked at each other in the mirror. He was, she thought, more beautiful than she'd ever been. Under his eyes were slight shadows which accentuated their shape: under hers were lines and crow's-feet. His lips pouted: hers were thin and surrounded by scores of fine lines. She did feel pangs, of regret and jealousy, but — She smiled and watched the lines under her eyes deepen. He was the one jumping through hoops. He couldn't yet afford to say, 'No,' and walk away. In a very short time, he would again be doing the interviews he hated. 'Let's face it, darling, you're not unpretty. And you know you love it, so don't gripe.'

He turned his back to the mirror. 'I wasn't picked just for looks, was I?'

'Of course you were, Sweet. They were going to have a computer-generated Dean, but I persuaded them you'd be cheaper.' She knew that to give reassurance was simply to comfirm that there was a need for reassurance. After that, it never stopped.

Reassured, he went to the couch and sprawled. She sat in a chair opposite, and crossed her legs. He stared at her. 'Black stockings and stilettos. You always look dead sexy.'

She smiled.

He stretched his arms above his head. Her company was comforting in itself – provided you knew she was on your side. No matter what happened, you knew she'd dealt with it before, and would deal with it again, without breaking step in her high-heels. She would chew up whoever got in her way, touch up her lipstick, and then turn to him and say, 'Darling, don't worry about it.'

He said, 'Can I show you something?'

'Darling. That depends on what.'

He was sitting, reaching for his jacket from the other end of the couch, but turned his head towards her, momentarily puzzled, before grinning. 'Not that. God, you've got a filthy mind.'

She crossed her legs. 'Ah me. It's always the fat old executives who flash me – never the gorgeous young leads.'

From the pocket of his jacket he'd taken a letter, which he tossed into her lap. The green envelope had already been torn open. The address was written in red ink. 'Oh-oh,' she said. 'Nutbag alert.' When he didn't laugh, she glanced up and saw him sitting on the edge of the couch, bent far forward over his knees. 'Oh,' she said.

She took the letter from its envelope and shook it out. Her spectacles hung round her neck on a string of amber beads, and she lifted them on to her nose and blinked at the letter.

Several pages of thin copy paper, so flimsy that the scrawl

on the sheets underneath could be seen through it, had been bulkily folded together. The words were in red ink, many in capital letters, many misspelt. Exclamation marks came plentifully, in twos and threes.

Half-way down the first page, she said, 'Oh dear me,' but went on reading. After another page she leaned her head on her extended forefinger, and flipped to the letter's end. '"Yours admiringly, a fan." Hmm.' She turned back to the beginning. 'No address.' She read a little more. 'He *does* have an imagination, doesn't he? I don't think I'll read any more.' She refolded the letter gingerly. 'You hardly like to touch it, do you, considering? I'll keep it and dispose of it for you. By incineration, I think. Darling, don't worry about it. This sort of thing comes with the territory. Now he's got this out of his system, you'll never hear from him again.'

'It makes me feel like he's coming up behind me.'

'Oh darling, I know. If you get any more, don't read them, just throw them in the trash.'

He spread his hands. 'They sell my address! In magazines. Send a cheque, we'll send you "the addresses of the stars"! And nutters like that send in their cheques and then write that stuff to me. How can they get off with selling my address? Is it legal?'

'I know, darling, I know, but it's just a letter.'

'The nutter who wrote it might drop by my room tonight.'

'No, darling. No. That *won't* happen.'

'It's not just him!' He jumped up and began to walk round the couch and her chair. 'My mom and dad had to move house – people were camping on their lawn and calling them all day and all night – they've had to move house! People were going through their garbage – they go through *my* garbage!'

'Darling–'

'Why do they *do* that? What do they want with my old beer cans and toe-nails and coffee-grounds?'

'Darling, don't get so worked up.'

'They send me presents. They send me cards and flowers and after-shave and chocolate and leather *g-strings*. I don't *know* them. What do they *want?*'

'I wish complete strangers would send *me* chocolates and perfume.'

'No you don't.' He dropped back on to the couch. 'If they did, you wouldn't.'

They sat still for a moment, looking at each other. 'Maybe not, darling. But that's fame for you. It's what you wanted, isn't it?'

'No! Well – I just wanted–' He started laughing and lay back full-length on the couch again. '– Not to have to work for a living.' She laughed with him, but his laughter soon stopped. 'I hate this, I hate it, hate it, hate it hate it.'

'Yes, well.' She opened her bag. Time to introduce some

mundane, routine little task, she thought. 'Can we do diaries a
moment, darling? Post-dubbing next month, you know that?'
There was a knock at the door and she raised her head. 'That'll
be room-service. Can you get it, Sweet?' She read through the
notes in her diary, while Will took the tray from the waiter
and tipped him. 'Pour me a glass of wine, there's a sweetheart
– and one for you, I don't want to drink alone. Let's relax and
put our feet up for a few minutes. But *eat* something.'

The clip of film ended and the screen went blank. From the
control room came Collucci's voice. 'Great, Will. At last. Want
to come through?'

Will took off the headphones, and pushed through the
double-doors into the control room.

'Want a cigarette?'

'That was great, Will.'

'Can I get you a coffee, Will?'

'Perfect, Will, spot on.'

Will was thinking that the voice-synching he had just done
was nowhere near as good as his original performance. So that
brought the whole performance down a notch. And all the
other scenes they had to voice-sync, because the sound
recording hadn't been up to scratch, were all going to damage
his performance a little bit more. It would be chipped away,
and chipped away, until all that was left would be the most

beautiful man in the world with a new haircut.

'Okay, I know it's late,' Collucci said, 'but the release date keeps getting closer. I want to do a couple more—'

'That means ten more,' said the man with the coffee.

'That okay with you, Will?'

'Can we do that again?' Will said. 'I mean, I want to take ten minutes, but—'

Collucci's face had frozen. Over Collucci's shoulder he saw dismay and contempt flicker over other faces. 'But I'd like to do that again.'

'It was *fine*, Will, it was perfect.'

'I'd like to do it again,' Will said.

'Wi-i-ll.' Collucci's hand moved to his shoulder. Will moved away. 'You want to stop before you take the edge off. Believe me, trust me, it was *perfect*.'

'I think I can do better.' He knew he could, but it was becoming a matter of winning his point.

'We'll see,' Collucci said. 'Sure, we'll see what we can do. How about you go and have your ten minutes? Ten minutes, not fifty – okay?'

He thinks I'm an idiot, Will thought, but he let it go, and pushed open the control-room's swing door. In the small lobby he deliberately lingered, listening, as the door swung slowly shut. He heard one of the technicians say, '*Je-ee-sus!* He wants to do it *again!*'

Will found his way through the corridors to the lift, and then through more silent, dim corridors and out of some side doors on to the lot.

Dusk was thickening in the grey roads between the grey offices and studios. Everything was losing its outlines, melting into a blur. He walked beside the wall of the sound studio, taking in a deep breath and letting it out long, throwing back his head and working his shoulders. He thought he would walk round two or three blocks before he went back, however long it took.

In his mind he planned a walk to his car, getting in, driving away . . . but the dubbing had to be done. Besides, think what they'd say. 'Who does he think he is, it's gone to his head, he believes his own publicity, he thinks he's a big star.' People fell over themselves to be the one to fetch him coffee he hadn't asked for and didn't want, but if he asked someone to pass him a pen, he was behaving like a prima-donna.

A car-engine crooned behind him. He stuck out his arm without bothering to look, his thumb up. Anywhere you're going, friend. I don't care.

He glanced back, and there was no car. The engine sound went on. He stopped, turned, looked – and the car emerged from the grey of the road and the ever-thickening dusk. A grey car – no, silver. A dusk-coloured car.

It crooned and ticked to a halt beside him. An old, classic

124

sports car, with sleek, rounded 'fifties styling. On its door, and on its dipped, oval bonnet was a large, rounded script number. 130. In the dim light the number looked black.

In the driving seat, bare arm along the car's door, lay a young man. His white t-shirt shone faintly in the dusk. Fair hair stood up stiffly above a wrinkling brow and a narrow, sharp-boned face. His eyes met Will's and, with a nod of his head, he indicated the empty seat beside him.

Will ran round the car and swung himself in over the door. As he settled in the seat, the car pulled away, snatching back his head. He forced his head up to see a grey road divided by a glimmering, stuttering white line streaking away into grey and darker grey and darkness. Telegraph poles flashed by – faster and faster – and the lines of poles narrowed, and the road, and the white line – faster, faster – and arrowed into the darkness ahead that had swallowed the road's distant point.

'Will?'

He was falling. His head jerked up, and he spun, and his reaching hand touched flat against the hard, warm wall behind him. He was standing in a narrow street among black blocks of buildings. Dusk was now dark.

'Hey, Will – Collucci says we're ready to go, okay?'

'Yeah? Yeah. Be right with you.'

'Will – great,' Collucci said, as Will came through the door.

'We're going with the motorbike scene – okay?'

It wasn't the scene he'd wanted to do again. Collucci evidently thought him too stupid to notice. 'Okay,' Will said, and went through the doors into the studio.

The technicians looked at each other. Collucci raised his brows. 'Gentlemen. We may get out of here tonight. Run the film.'

'So, Will – can I get away with mentioning your latest award?'

'What award?'

'Didn't you see? Here – you've been voted "Best Body of the Year".'

'Yeah? That's cool.'

'You know, I was warned – "Don't, whatever you do, mention that 'Most Beautiful Man in the World' business. He goes ballistic."'

'So you mention it, right? It's fine. Gotta be better than being voted Ugliest Shit-Face of the Year.'

'It used to get to you. But now you've learned to deal with it, right?'

'No.'

'No?'

'It's just — Who cares?'

It was a private screening of the film, for studio executives, their guests, and the various interested parties who always managed to inveigle their way into such affairs. Debs was among them.

The film flickered through the darkness on to the screen. From the seats in front of her came the little shiftings, the sighs, the rubbings of cloth on seats of this intent and highly sensitised audience. Nobody knew anything, of course, but the antennae of this audience quivered to catch every nuance of possible success or failure. They felt it in their *wallets*.

For perhaps fifteen minutes she sensed, in the shufflings, the coughs, the silence, a resistance – the wariness and suspicion of, probably, the most hostile audience the film would ever face. That was their livelihood at risk up there on the screen.

And then there was a warming. Chairs creaked as people stretched and lay back. The silence began to be broken by quiet laughter, and whispered comments which sounded appreciative. She saw heads, silhouetted against the screen's light, lean together and nod.

Someone said, 'This has got to be a winner.'

Debs nodded to herself in the dark. The film was a winner. Not the greatest money-maker of the year: it didn't have enough explosions, gun-fire and blood for that. But it was going to get good reviews, and would go on earning, through video and TV, for years and years.

She hated it. As everyone else in the room relaxed, and the

sense of congratulation strengthened, she felt isolated, as if she was shut inside a little glass box.

She felt like going to the producer, the director and saying, 'So you used the computer after all. What have you done with Will?'

There was his face on the screen, so well-lit that in three separate scenes even she – who knew very well how red-eyed, bovine and plain he could look in the flesh – was astonished by his beauty. There were his mannerisms – a particular way of inclining his head, a certain, often used inflection of his voice.

But where was *Will?*

It couldn't be said his acting was bad. He wasn't wooden. He wasn't ham. He just wasn't there.

From a row or two in front, where the silvery beams cut through the darkness and danced over the heads, a woman's voice came back to her. 'Y'know . . . I really think he might be the most beautiful man in the world.' There was soft, appreciative laughter in the dark.

Debs got up and went outside. In the brilliant light of a glass-walled corridor, she blinked among the potted plants. There was no question but that she'd go on working just as hard for Will . . .

At least until other people starting noticing that he'd gone missing.

She ran a business, not a charity.

But it was astonishing on how little some careers could be maintained. In this business nobody knew anything. And Will would be needing a friend.

She hoped he had one.

Cold Silver

It was Midsummer's Eve. The brightness of the pale blue sky had dimmed only a little, and both the sun and the moon were up – the sun a yellow, sinking ball, and the moon a flimsy grey-white nail-clipping.

The little forge was open on one side. Its three walls of damp, moss-grown, crumbling brick leaned together like those of a card-house. Inside, on a big iron anvil, lay a silver horseshoe. The holes had been punched through it, ready for the nails. Silver nails. Not the silver of hammer-polished iron, but real silver, cold-worked. The shoe's hammer-marked surface caught the evening light in ripples. Aidan stood looking down at it, then flicked his cigarette ash across it and went out of the forge.

A couple of yards away, the river ran by, broad and powerfully slow, black, green and whispering. The river hung on to the day, catching and redoubling the light. Brownish clouds of gnats hovered above the water and Aidan blew smoke at them as, humming faintly, they came to whirl round him.

Even there, by the water, even at that hour, as the long

summer day finally faded into evening, it was hot. The air was warm on the skin, thick to breathe, and full of scents: the wet earth of the riverbank and the green smells of grass and leaves.

The land sloped up from the river in rough meadows of thick, tussocky grass, broken by stands of trees and ill-kept hedges. Darkness already gathered in the shelter of their leaves. Beyond them, rising against the western sky, was a hill. Miss Lanark said there was a barrow up there: an ancient grave of ancient kings.

The sun dipped closer to the hill, turning orange as it sank, and the blue of the sky dimmed to indigo. In the darkest part of the sky, the moon's crescent shone a clearer white.

The loudest sound under the moon was silence. Aidan came from a town where the noise of traffic never stopped. Silence of this strength was strange to him, and he stood smoking and listening to it reverberate across the darkening fields, running deep under the quiet of the river, deep under the ruffling of the leaves.

There was nobody near him. Stretching out on every side were empty fields, hunted through and over by owls and foxes. He had to stay there, all night long, alone, waiting for 'those who come by'.

Inside his own head, to himself, he could admit what he would never admit to anyone else, not even his girl, not even his granddad. He didn't like being there. He didn't like the stifling quiet, nor the fact that there was no one about to help if anything – God knew what – went wrong. He didn't like the fact that it was getting darker.

He wished he'd brought a Gameboy, or a magazine.

'What's the weirdest job you've ever done?' At least, in future, he'd always have an answer for that.

He threw away his cigarette and, as the smell of tobacco faded, a strong honey-scent drifted to him, coming and going in the air. Late may-blossom or wild honeysuckle was growing somewhere near, its scent coaxed out by the warmth and the evening. He even thought he could smell the old, burned out clinkers of the forge-fire, and hot iron – but there hadn't been a fire in that old forge for years. It was too clean. That smell was coming from his memory. It was odd to work a forge without a fire, without the stench of burning coke, and the tang of red-hot, cooling iron, and so his imagination was supplying the smells. But, although it seemed all wrong, he was glad not to add the fiercer heat of fire to this hot evening.

The sun dropped below the hill, leaving the sky polished gold above it. Above and around the gold, the pink turned to just the sullen red of coals in a forge-fire. Darkness came quickly then. Colour went from the grass and trees around him, surrounding him with vague, soft, grey shapes – and depths of silence.

Now the moon was bone-white, gathering strength from

the dark. All detail had gone from the land round him. There was no telling if that was a bush over there, growing by that tree, or just the tree's shadow, or someone standing there, stooped over.

He went back to the forge and switched on his battery lamp. Its bright, hard light glared on the close things: the lime flaking from the brick walls, the old cinders trodden into the earth floor; the cobwebs hanging from the wooden rafters under the slate roof; the dull iron of the hood over the hearth's cold bricks. The shadows cast were as hard-edged and black as the light was bright. The moment the light snapped on, the darkness outside became blacker too: but a deep, soft blackness. The trees, hedges, everything, sank into it and vanished.

On the dark anvil a crescent moon lay shining: the silver horseshoe. He sat on the anvil, his bare knee poking through a hole in his jeans, and picked the horseshoe up, turning it round in his hands. On the splintered old bench behind the anvil lay a heap of rough-made horseshoes and their nails, all silver. He'd spent the day making them.

'Silver horseshoes,' he'd said. 'Much use as a chocolate teapot.'

'*Has* to be silver, poppet,' Miss Lanark had yelled. 'It's tradition, like mince-pies at Christmas and eggs at Easter.' She was one of those loud-voiced posh women – he'd shoed horses for enough of them – who called you 'poppet' and, behind your back, said you were 'her little man'. A nice enough old bint, but—

Mad as a boiled owl, for one thing.

And rolling in it. She owned all this land by the river – she owned the hill with the barrow. He knew, because she'd said people wanted to dig it up and she wouldn't give them permission. 'And if I ever catch anyone up there with a metal-detector, I shall *shoot* them.'

She'd provided all this silver. A hundred rods of it, all just the right size and thickness to be quickly hammered into horseshoes. Must have cost a fortune.

'Somebody's got to keep up these traditions,' she said. 'You eat mince-pies at Christmas, don't you? Build bonfires on November the fifth? You look to me like a young chap who'd build a good bonfire.'

She lived alone in this big house with about ten bedrooms, and she'd put him up in one with its own bathroom attached. 'I'll take good care of him,' she'd said, to his dad and granddad, 'and I promise you on my honour I won't molest him.' His dad had been shocked, and his granddad hadn't known where to put himself after hearing a woman say such a thing. Aidan would have thought it was funny, if she hadn't been talking about him as if he was a little kid. But he couldn't hold it too much against her. For this one day and one night of work, she was paying him a week's wages, plus expenses and board.

Not that he wasn't earning it. A whole boring bloody night in the middle of a field in the middle of bloody nowhere. And bloody silver horseshoes.

He found out why she'd asked him to come a day early when he'd arrived, and she'd taken him out to the forge, and produced the silver rods from the boot of her big estate car. 'I don't suppose you've ever worked silver, have you, poppet?'

Her posh accent grated. 'There bay never bin much call,' he'd said, speaking broader than his granddad, 'for silver hoss-shoes. Not in our neck of the woods, Shuck.'

Well, she'd said, she was no smith herself of course, but her old farrier – a dear little man, but he'd died, alas – had made the silver up into horseshoes in a trice! He hadn't used a fire, if that was any help.

'It works cold?' Aidan had said and, twitching his cigarette from one corner of his mouth to the other, had tried one of the rods between his hands. 'I'll gi' it a goo.'

He'd spent the day practising, and had found that the cold silver shaped easily under the hammer. He had to be quick and light, though – too much hammering turned the metal brittle and it cracked. He ruined a few shoes before he got the hang of it. After that, he made up the roughs, and finished the one, right down to the nail-holes, just to show it could be done. The hammer sounded strange, though – muffled and dull, muttering, 'Wrong, wrong,' with every blow, instead of

136

hard iron's ringing cry of 'Good work! Good work!'

Still, he was proud of his silver horseshoe, useless as it was. His dad and granddad had made way more horseshoes than he'd had days alive, but neither one of them had ever made a silver horseshoe. Sitting on the anvil, he held up the shoe and squinted at the moon through the nail-holes. For a while he held the shoe up before the moon and tried to fit the silver crescent to the moon's curve. But the shapes wouldn't fit.

Miss Lanark had been pleased, that afternoon, when she'd seen his heap of rough shoes. 'Splendid!' she'd said. 'I can see why "Dad" and "Granddad" are so proud of you!' He'd set his teeth. On the first day they'd met, months ago, when she'd come to their yard to ask them to do this weird job for her, she'd heard him call his father and grandfather 'Dad' and 'Granddad', and it had amused her, for some reason. Ever since, even on that same day, she'd called them 'Dad' and 'Granddad' too, even to their faces, and always with a little spin on the words that he didn't like. As if she was making fun of them. Or of him. 'Help me get the shoes into the boot, and then I'll take you and buy you a very big dinner somewhere. I shan't need to get you back here until ten at the earliest.'

He'd said, 'Does anybody else know I'm going to be out here on me own with all this silver?' It was something that had been worrying him as he'd sweated over cold-working the silver in broad daylight, out in the middle of that lonely field.

Nobody had come by, all the long hot day.

'Private land,' she said. 'Don't worry, poppet. No one comes by here much.'

Then what's tonight all about? he'd wanted to ask. But what the hell. If she wanted him to sit all night in a field, he would, for the kind of money she was paying.

After the meal, on the drive to the forge, she'd suddenly said, 'Did I say that you weren't to speak, at all, all night?'

He threw a cigarette-stub from the car's open window. 'Doe sound like there'll be any bug–beggar to spake to.'

'Not a word spoken, all through the night,' she'd said. ' "And the smith, to shoe with silver the horses of those who come by." '

He'd been thinking about actually trying to hammer a silver shoe on to a horse's hoof with silver nails. 'Has anybody ever come by?'

'Have you got a jacket with you? You won't be warm enough in just that thin t-shirt.'

'It's warm.'

'It's warm now. It'll get cold in the early morning.' And when they'd reached the forge, she'd leaned into the back of the car and dragged out a big padded jacket, covered in stains and dog-hairs. 'Have this of mine. Believe me, you'll be glad of it.'

'Woe fit me.'

'Oh, it *will*. Great Scot, I'd make two of you.'

He took it from her, to save argument, and threw it on to the workbench. He wouldn't need it, and even if he did, it wouldn't fit him. She might outweigh him, but her coats weren't cut for a blacksmith's arms and shoulders.

'And here's a present for you.' From somewhere in the car she'd produced a four-pack of beer. 'Oh! That's earned me a smile!'

'Thanks, Miss Lanark.' He'd broken out one bottle straight away, to show that he appreciated it. She'd helped him carry the silver shoes and his tools into the forge, and had told him again, several times, that he mustn't speak all night through. His teeth were gritted by the time she'd got back into her car, blown him a kiss, shouted, ' 'Bye, sweetie!' and had driven off down the track.

He'd watched her go, let out a long sigh, and lit up a cigarette to celebrate. A nice enough old duck, but bossy, loud, mad as a boiled owl and a bit of a nag. He'd be glad to see the back of her for a while.

He sat astride the anvil and looked out at the wall of blackness and silence beyond his bright electric light. Ducking his head, he lit another cigarette, cupping his hand about the flame so that his face was sheltered from the light of the electric lamp and goldenly lit by the match. Lifting his head and shaking out the match, he kicked up the anvil –

and was startled by a horse's whinny.

He jumped down and swung round the doorpost into the dark. The whinny had come from the fields, and most of the light from the electric lamp spilled out of the forge's open side towards the river. He squinted into the dark, but his eyes were dazzled by the electric light and all he could see was the black shape of the hill against the blue-grey, moon-washed sky. He cocked his head, listening.

And heard a creaking and a faint bell-ringing of metal, a cool sound in the dusk. He knew the sounds: riders shifting in saddles, and the bits ringing. People riding, over rough ground like this, in the dark? Just to keep some half-baked tradition? They had to be crazy. He stood by the forge, one hand on its still warm brick, and listened. He heard a horse snort, and then the swish of long grass brushing against the horse's legs. It was a moment or two before it occurred to him that he couldn't hear the hooves on the turf.

Midnight now, at least, and it was getting colder. He rubbed his bare arms.

Out of the dark, glimmering, first grey, then white, came a horse. The moonlight struck a metallic gleam from its rider's head and chest. Behind the white horse were others, movements of mass in the dark: quiet ringing of bridles, creaking of harness. On they came to the forge.

Long beams of light shining through chinks in the forge

walls shone dull on iron helmets, on a chestnut flank, a chequered saddle-blanket. Astonished, Aidan looked up at the men who swayed in the saddles and turned their shadowed faces down to him. A shiver struck through him and he hugged himself with both arms, feeling his skin rough with goosebumps. The air was cold now: thick and damp, clinging round him. He couldn't smell the horses, though they were so close. All he could smell – and it was as if he had opened the earth of his granddad's garden with a spade – was wet earth, and clay and age.

The white horse, right by him, shook its head and blew down its nose, its bridle ringing. He felt the breath on his arm, a double, cold jet. The chill of it went through him to his spine. The horses loomed all round him now, saddles creaking, tails flicking – but he had not heard a hoof strike the ground.

He looked down. In a shaft of light from the forge, a rim of silver gleamed on a hoof. A horse shifted, raising its foot and setting it down again – and never touched the earth.

Silver horseshoes are as much use as chocolate teapots – to horses that walk on the ground.

He thrust out his hand and touched the shoulder of the white horse. He felt the harshness of its hair, felt its flesh yield to his touch, and then the resistance of its deep muscles – but there was none of a horse's warmth. Touching this horse chilled his hand with a bite, as if he had pressed it to ice.

He lifted his head, looking up at the rider —

As quickly, the rider leaned down and pressed fingers to Aidan's mouth, flattening his lips against his teeth. The fingers were hard, and cold, and smelled of earth.

He wasn't to speak. Here were darkness and moonshine, woven through the stands of trees and the wide silence of the fields. One spoken word could tear it apart.

Aidan nodded that he understood, and the rider straightened in his saddle, drawing back his hand. His cold touch stayed on Aidan's mouth.

The rider swung down from his horse, and with a rustling and creaking, every rider swung down, and the horses were led forward, without a hoof-beat, down the slope to the river. They pushed through the bushes and grass, breaking leaves and crushing stems, releasing juice and green scents. The bits rattled and rang as the horses shook their heads, and the steady running murmur of the river was broken by the splashing, dimpling and ringing as the horses lipped the water, raised their dripping heads and shook their manes. The dim light thrown up from the rippling water glimmered among the overhanging branches.

Aidan had gone to his forge, and was sticking the tools he would need into the waistband of his jeans. He was ready when the first chestnut was led up. Its flank gleamed in the electric lamp's hard white light, and cold rose from its body. A man was at the horse's head. Aidan moved to the horse's side, too shy to look at the man. He lifted its forefoot, gripping it between his knees, and levered off the old shoe with his paring-knife, drawing out the nails with it. Before he threw it aside, he turned it in his hand, looking at it. It was worn thin as a sixpence – as his granddad would say.

As the old horseshoe hit the ground, Aidan was scraping out the hoof, and paring it down. He was trying not to shiver. Where his side touched the horse, its touch first chilled him, and then soaked through his thin cotton t-shirt and sank into his ribs and back. The hoof was cold the way metal is cold, and was chilling his hands as he worked. Setting the horse's foot down, he went back to the anvil to fetch one of the rough shoes. Returning and lifting the foot again, he checked the fit, noting with his eye where the shape differed and needed the hammer.

He set the foot down again and straightened. The muscles of his chilled side were slow, and though he moved as quickly and easily as ever, he felt it, and thought of his granddad.

The forge was surrounded by horses now, some in the light, some mere shapes in the dark. Men stood at their heads, or leaned on the forge walls. From them, the cold reached out.

Aidan moved through them, to the anvil. With each one he passed, he felt the warmth drain from him to them. Now he wished that he had built a fire in the forge. The men moved aside for him, nodding to him, the smith, but never speaking. Too shy to look at them directly, he glanced at them sidelong, and saw the light catch on dull iron rings sewn to scuffed leather. A brighter gleam showed a brooch at a shoulder. On a face turning into the light he saw a hairless scar dividing a beard. A fall of chequered cloak was strange in its very weave and texture, rough and knubbly, its edges frayed with use.

Aidan took up the hammer and felt the men lean to watch. The cold closed closer round him, and their silence was deeper than the silence of the fields. He kept his eyes on his work, hammering, matching the shape of the shoe to the shape of the hoof in his memory, using the punch to make the nail-holes. When he finished and stepped away from the anvil, he looked up and saw many faces turned towards him, even if their features were hidden in darkness. Eyes caught the light with a flat, dull shine.

Even in so short a time, he had forgotten how sharp the cold was until he bent to the horse's foot again, and felt the chill strike through his side into his innards. His fingers clung stickily to the cold hoof. It was a temptation, when the fit of the shoe seemed fair enough, to fix it on and have done, to get away from that cold. How good a fit did it have to be for a horse that never trod on the ground? But the old shoe had worn thin against something. 'Do a good job', said his dad and granddad in his head, and for them, and for their pride in him, he took the shoe back to the anvil and shaped it again. After all, this cold shoe couldn't burn its way to a good fit. He filled his mouth with nails before going back to the horse, and God, that horse got colder every time he touched it. He was starting to shiver. He held the cold hoof between his knees and hammered in the nails, expecting them to bend uselessly. But they went in like good 'uns, and he clinched them down, filed them, and let the horse's hoof down.

He moved round the horse to its other forefoot, and he was shivering continually – dithering, his granddad would say. An occasional strong shiver would rattle his teeth together. Now he was at the horse's other side, it was his other side that was chilled, and he was becoming cold through and through. But he lifted the foot, pried off its old, thin shoe and cleaned up its hoof.

He went back to the anvil to fetch another shoe, and edged through the silent, watching men, trying not to look at them. He was beginning to long to hear someone speak, but he was too shy even if it hadn't been forbidden. He wondered if these men could speak. Their cold hung in the air like fog, settling on him. In the forge, he reached over the anvil for the padded jacket he had thrown on the workbench. It was as he'd thought: the body was too big and flapped about him, but the shoulders and arms were tight. It would be hard to work in it – at first.

He needed the warmth, and the seams would give before his shoulders did.

Miss Lanark, it occurred to him, knew more than she'd been telling.

He'd tell his granddad that he'd shoed horses on Midsummer Eve while shivering with cold. That would make the old man laugh. Then he thought that he wouldn't ever be able to tell anyone about this: cold fingers had closed his mouth.

He had the measure of the shoe in his head now, and did some of the reshaping before he went back to the horse and tried it on the hoof. For the first few seconds, he thought the padded jacket was protecting him against the cold; but while he was nailing the shoe, he felt the deep chill sinking painfully through his ribs again.

He removed the horse's third shoe, cleaned up its hoof, and, as he went back to the anvil, looked round and tried to count the horses waiting. He couldn't see well into the darkness beyond the glare of white electric light. But there were more than five horses: that much he'd seen as they'd gone down to the river. How am I going to get through this? he wondered. By the time he was nailing on the fourth shoe, he was dithering even in the jacket. As the big chestnut was led away silently in its new silver shoes, and another horse – a bay – was led into the lamplight, Aidan stepped away from the forge and lit a cigarette.

If the night was still warm, he couldn't feel it. He cupped his hands about the match and let it burn. He could feel the tiny heat of the flame on his skin, but it was as if he was enclosed in a second skin of cold and through it the heat reached him faintly. When the match burned out in his chilled fingers, he hardly felt the smart.

He went back into the harsh white light around the forge, and bent to the forefoot of the bay horse. Turning its head, it snorted cold breath down his back. Hot ash and tiny red sparks spilled from his cigarette on to his cold hands, reminding him of his forge-fire, and the sparks that flew from his hot, beaten iron.

Bending to lift the heavy hoofs, gripping them between his knees, levering off the old shoes, drawing out the nails with them. All the time using twice the necessary strength in controlling his own shivering. Cleaning and paring the hoof. Taking the cold shoe from his waistband and trying it for fit; and then the hammering at the anvil, gripping the hammer-shaft, soaking up the jarring of the blows. Bending his cold back again to lift the heavy hoof again, leaning on the horse's cold side. Hammering home the nails, clinching, filing, setting the hoof down – and there was another heavy hoof to lift.

The cold was a strait-jacket on his every movement: his muscles strained against it, feeling bruised. He had to shape and reshape his grip on his tools, striving to use them with stiffening fingers. He stopped noticing or counting the horses. Some stood more patiently than others, that was all he cared. Cold was what he thought of: cold, and how long he could keep going, and whether he could finish the job. The cold had seeped so far through him that his bones ached with it and were heavy to move. His head ached; his teeth ached. But he had a job to finish.

He set down, for the last time, the last foot of a white horse and, with effort, straightened his back. There was a tightening band of cold about his head as he turned to look about. His hands were cramped, with cold and effort, to the shape of his tools, and his legs and arms trembled with the repeated blows. He was looking about for the next horse.

Someone struck his shoulder. He was so cold, the blow hurt, and he felt that it might have shattered him, like ice. He turned, and saw the man who had struck him swinging up into a saddle. Further away, at the edge of the white light and the darkness, the shapes of other riders could be seen, in the saddle, or mounting up. They were leaving. The job was finished.

The white horse loomed cold beside and above him. He looked up at the rider on its back, and saw the iron shine of the helmet above the shadowed face. A hand was held out and down to him. Shaking, from cold or the hammer, Aidan reached up and took something hard from the hand. His sense of touch was too dulled by cold for him to tell what it was: except that it was hard and round.

The horseman's cold fingers pressed hard to his mouth again – almost before Aidan himself knew that he had been going to speak. No word was to be said, even in thanks or goodbye.

The white horse was kicked up, and the other riders let it take the lead, before falling in behind. They rode out of the lamp's bright light, into the twilight beyond, and then into the dark, towards the hill that rose unseen against the western sky. No hoof-falls came back to him.

Aidan went to the forge wall, leaned against it and slid down it until he was sitting on the ground. He was so bruised and stiff with cold that he could no longer shiver. The trembling that ran through him was from the weariness of gripping the hammer so long, and absorbing the jarring of the many, many blows. He drew up his knees and huddled in the jacket, pushing his hands under his armpits. His head he leaned on his knees, closing his eyes. Inside his head, his mind ran round and round. Midsummer night, it said: four hours from midnight to dawn. He tried to remember how many horses he had shoed, or how many riders there had been, but he had never counted them and could only guess. Too many, and more than four hours' work. But it was still dark.

He heard the first twitters of birds, and opened his eyes to see that his lamp's light was becoming lost in the twilight of early morning. He remembered that he'd been given something. He took his hand from inside the jacket, still clenched about the gift. His fingers were so cold, he had to use his other hand to open them out. In his palm lay a big ring.

Clumsily, he took it between finger and thumb. If it wasn't gold . . . A knot of wires, twisting in and out, over and over. He dropped the ring as he tried to turn it. Picking it out of the folds of the jacket, he tilted it, watching the light run over the metal and following the twists with his eyes. It made him feel dizzy, the endless circling and looping with no beginning or end, but he began to see how it could be made. In copper wire he could make – well, something like it. His first effort wouldn't be worth much. Round and round he followed the working of the ring, as the light on it brightened and his eyes hardly blinked, round and round. He'd never worked gold, but then, he'd never worked silver before either . . .

It was something after six in the morning when Miss Lanark drove her Range-Rover along the riverside track. The sky was high, blue and cloudless, and though not yet hot, the day was already warm enough for her to be comfortable in shirtsleeves. As she drew up near the forge, she could see the boy slumped against its wall, wearing her quilted, padded jacket.

A flask and a blanket lay on the passenger seat beside her.

She tucked them under her arm before getting out, calling, 'Morning!' The boy was staring at something in his hand, and didn't look round or answer her.

She went over and crouched beside him, setting the blanket and flask on the ground. It was a ring he held, a big thing. She could see the earth encrusted in the grooves of it. He stared at it without so much as a flicker of the eye to give away that he knew she was there – though he must have known she was there.

She put her own hand over the ring, hiding it from his sight – and felt, with a shiver, how very cold his hand was. He did lift his eyes and look at her, once he couldn't see the ring. He looked at her as if he didn't believe in her. She put the back of her hand to his cheek and was shocked at how hard and cold his skin was. Like iron in winter.

'Come on!' she said, and shook out the blanket and wrapped it round him, pulling him away from the wall as she tucked it behind him. He let her sway him this way and that – he was staring at the ring again.

Crouching beside him again, she opened the flask and poured hot tomato soup into the lid. The smell, she thought, would wake him up – but no: the ring was too fascinating.

'Can I see that, poppet? May I?' She snatched the ring out of his fingers, and put it in the pocket of her shirt. He stared round for it, dazed. She put the cup of hot soup into his hand, fastening his fingers round it. Even then she had to lift his hand and the cup towards his face before he seemed to notice it, but then he did drink.

She stayed and watched him drink half the cup, and then refilled it from the flask, before going to gather up the old, worn horseshoes, to throw them into the boot of the car. As she passed to and fro, he watched her, staring over the rim of the cup. She had no doubt that he was thinking of the ring.

When she'd packed all his tools away in the boot, she went back to him. He looked up as she came near and seemed about to speak. 'Mmm?' she said.

His mouth opened, and he made a slight gulping motion of the head, as if gagging, but made no sound. Despite the hot soup, he was still cold through, and his tongue seemed locked in ice.

'Finish that drop of soup,' she said. 'Then we'll get you back to the house. I promised "Dad" and "Granddad" I'd look after you, didn't I?'

It was hard getting up. Cold had stiffened him in every joint. He moved to the car like an old man. Miss Lanark shut the passenger door on him, and got in the other side. She had to fasten his safety belt because his fingers could only fumble at it.

'A hot shower, a hot meal,' she said, hoping she was right, 'and you'll be skipping like a spring lamb, you'll see.'

He swallowed, and tried hard to work his tongue loose. His throat moved, but the words wouldn't come. The sealing chill of the cold fingers still lay across his mouth. The car jolted and bounced almost the length of the track, was almost at the entrance to the lane, before he managed, through an uncleared throat. 'My ring!'

'How charming your dulcet tones, my love!' Miss Lanark was relieved. God knew, the boy was never exactly chatty, but she'd begun to be unnerved by his dazed, silent stares.

'My ring,' he said.

She didn't want to fumble in her shirt-pocket while she was driving and, anyway, he had been so unhandy with the safety-belt that he would probably drop it, and it would roll under the seats. 'I'll give it to you at the house.'

'Want it,' he said.

'Have another sandwich.'

'I want my ring.'

She braked at the entrance to the lane, took the ring from her pocket and, leaning over to him, stuck it on his thumb. Immediately he relaxed, leaning back in his seat and staring at it.

'You should get it valued,' she said, once she'd pulled out into the lane. 'It's old. You earned it.'

Aidan was holding the ring close to his face, squinting at some detail of its construction. Her words went past him. He would never have it valued, wasn't interested in its age or its value. He was planning to take it apart, the better to see how it was made.

He cleared his throat and said, 'Miss Lanark?'

'Yes, Poppet?' Now he was craning forward to see something ahead of them. She was glad to see him taking an interest in something other than the ring.

'Next year—'

'Yes? Next year?'

'I'm your smith.'

'Poppet! That's sweet of you.' As she ducked her head to get a better look at a road junction ahead, she saw what it was he stared at. In the blue, early morning sky there still hung, like a grey-white nail-clipping, the midsummer moon.

' . . . *Every Midsummer Eve, King Arthur and his knights come out of the mound . . . on horses shod with silver . . .*' From Katherine Briggs' A DICTIONARY OF BRITISH FOLK-TALES.